Rosecliff Manor Haunting

An Addison Lockhart Novella (Book 2)

New York Times & USA Today
Bestselling Author

Cheryl Bradshaw

This book is a work of fiction. Names, characters, places, businesses, and incidents either are the products of the author's imagination or are used in a fictitious manner. Any similarity to events or locales or persons, living or dead, is entirely coincidental.

No part of this publication may be reproduced, stored or transmitted, in any form, or by any means whatsoever (electronic, mechanical, etc.) without the prior written permission and consent of the author.

First edition May 2015
Copyright © 2015 by Cheryl Bradshaw
Cover Design Copyright 2015 © Indie Designz
Interior book design by Bob Houston eBook Formatting
All rights reserved.

ISBN-13: 978-1511815796
ISBN-10: 1511815795

ACKNOWLEDGEMENTS

It took two years to publish this second book in the Addison Lockhart series, so I'd first like to thank the fans for graciously waiting so long for its arrival. When I wrote book one, Grayson Manor Haunting, I had no idea it would develop a cult following. It's been exciting to see fans take to this series in the same way they've taken to my other series.

To my husband for always supporting my career and my passion. Janet Green (thewordverve), who is like ten people rolled into one-thank you for always making my work shine. Amy Jirsa-Smith and Jenx Byron for noticing all the gaffes I tend to glaze over. To Bob Houston for excellent formatting and Dafeenah Jameel for making every single thing I do look like a spectacular masterpiece. To Elizabeth Winick Rubinstein for always being there and for taking my work to new heights. To Karen Tobias for assisting with legal questions and D.P. Lyle for your forensic evidence support. Finally, the hauntingly beautiful theme song of this novella is "Sweet Afton" by Nickel Creek.

"I claim not to have controlled events,
but confess plainly that events have controlled me."

-Abraham Lincoln

CHAPTER 1

Addison Lockhart's eyes blinked open, and she glanced around, surprised to find herself standing next to a tall, wrought-iron gate lining the perimeter in front of a three-story manor. She didn't know where she was, how long she'd been there, or how she came to be there in the first place. It was like she'd been transported through time, sucked through one end of a static passageway and spit out the other.

Ten minutes earlier, it was nighttime, and she was at home, although she couldn't recall what she'd been doing before she'd been plucked away. Now it was daytime, and the sun's delicate rays enveloped her, pulsing shots of heat through every pore of her freckled skin.

Addison looked around. Besides the manor, there were a few other houses in view, but the neighborhood was quiet. Almost too quiet. No birds chirping. No dogs barking. No wind. No noticeable sounds of any kind.

The noise wasn't all that was lacking either. When she glanced down she gasped, finding herself dressed in a practically see-through nightgown. Her feet were bare, her exposed arms and legs a milkier shade of white than she remembered them being.

None of it made sense.

A car turned down the road, and her eyes darted around, desperate to find a hiding spot to shield her half-naked body. She wrapped her fingers around the rails of the gate in front of her and pushed forward. But the gate wouldn't budge, and the car was fast approaching. Having no other place to go, she crossed her arms in front of her breasts, squeezed her legs together, and hoped for the best.

The car passed by like it was gliding on air, silent, and without stopping. The man in the driver's seat couldn't have been more than four feet away, and yet, he never looked over. Not even a single fleeting glance. Addison stared in disbelief as he coasted by. His chocolate brown hair was long and feathered, and the car he was driving, an orange Ford coupe with black stripes, looked out of place considering it was 2015.

The car didn't belong.

And he didn't belong.

Or maybe it was the other way around.

Maybe *she* was the one who was out of place.

Addison watched the car disappear over the other side of the hill and then turned, shifting her focus back to the manor, a smoky gray building with eight symmetrical windows lining the first two levels. The home's exterior looked like it had been carved from a single slab of stone, except for the thick, wooden door in the center. She stared at the door for a moment, and two things happened: a wave of sound penetrated the stale air like a needle pricking a balloon, and the front door of the manor creaked opened. Two girls spilled out, both wearing yellow, short-sleeved dresses with Peter Pan collars.

The door closed behind the twin girls as they descended a series of steps in front of the house, both hopping off the last one onto the meticulously mowed grass in the front yard. One of the girls squatted, picking a thin tree branch off the ground. She slapped the wood against her flat hand, innocently taunting her twin before waving the stick in the air. The twin, who held a furry, white kitten in her arms, pressed it against her chest like the cat's life depended on it.

The girl with the stick used it as a wand, pointing and taunting in the other girl's direction. "You better run, Grace, or the cat gets it!"

"You wouldn't, Viv!" the other girl shrieked.

And the chase was on, both girls circling the trunk of a majestic oak several times before an out-of-breath Grace sagged to the ground, relenting. She looked at Viv. "You better not hurt Shadow. I mean it!"

Viv rolled her eyes and plopped down beside her, tossing the stick across the yard. "Don't blow your top, Grace. I'd never hurt her, and you know it."

Grace squinted, screwing up her face at Viv like she wasn't sure whether she believed her. "Oh…kay. Why'd ya chase me with a stick then?"

"Good grief, I was just teasin'." Viv tipped her head toward the cat. "Thought you wanted to play hopscotch."

"I do."

"Why don't you put the fur ball down then?"

Grace surveyed the area. "Out here? I can't. What if she gets out of the yard and gets hit by a car? Or what if she runs away and we can't find her? Or what if—"

Viv held a flattened hand out in front of her. "All right, all right. I get it. Put her back in the house then."

Grace stroked the cat, frowned. "Can't I just hold her and play?"

Viv sighed. "Fine. But if we're gonna do it, let's get on with it."

Addison crossed her arms in front of her, watching the girls' long, blond, pigtails bob up and down while they hopped along the chalk squares on the driveway. She wondered if they saw her watching them from outside the gate but the few times they glanced in her direction, they looked past her like she wasn't there.

In an effort to find out where she was and how she got there, Addison cupped a hand over the side of her mouth and shouted, "Hello?"

No response.

She tried again. "Excuse me. Girls. Can you hear me?"

Again, no response.

She stood for several seconds, frustrated and confused before a glaring oversight occurred to her. Nothing about this place made sense. The people, the air, the colors, the car. Everything was off somehow. Everything was ... wrong.

Am I ... dreaming?

The more she thought about it, the more she convinced herself it was true.

That's it. This is a dream. It has to be. No one sees me because none of this is real.

It made sense because it had to. And because there was no other possible explanation for what she was experiencing. Now to prove the theory.

Addison pinched the flesh on her arm with the tips of her fingernails. Nothing. No pain. No sensation.

Come on, Addison ... wake up.

She squeezed her eyes shut then opened them, finding herself still there, trapped in her own twisted version of the *Twilight Zone*.

She leaned her head against the gate, and even considered banging against it a few times. Why not? It wasn't like she'd hurt anything.

"Hi."

The word was uttered in such a hush Addison almost didn't hear it. She looked down. One of the twins stood on the opposite side of the gate, her face pensive, eyes curious. The second twin was nowhere in sight.

"Hi," Addison replied.

"My name is Vivian. What's yours?"

"Addison. You can see me?"

"Of course I can see you," the girl said. "We both can."

And yet when Addison had called out to them just moments ago, neither of them responded. Interesting.

"The other girl. She's your twin sister, right?"

Vivian nodded. "Her name's Grace."

"Where is she?"

"She's hiding."

"Why?"

"She's afraid."

Addison reached out, attempting to place a hand on Vivian's shoulder. Vivian jerked back. Message received.

"Oh, honey," Addison said. "Your sister doesn't need to be afraid. Neither of you do."

Vivian shrugged. "She didn't want you to come."

"Come where?"

"Come here."

Still unsure of where *here* was, Addison decided not to push it. "Why not?"

"No one has ever seen us before."

No one had ever seen them? How could that be possible?

The kitten leapt out from behind a bush next to the manor. Grace chased after it, yelling, "Shadow, no! Stop!"

But the tenacious feline bounded forward. Vivian intercepted it, snatching the kitten up in one hand before it slipped past the gate. She walked over to Grace and deposited the cat back into her arms. Whispers between the two girls followed, too low for Addison to hear. Grace then tugged at the layers of fabric on Vivian's dress, like she was trying to hold her back, keep her from returning to the gate again.

Vivian escaped Grace's grasp, walked halfway back to the gate, and stopped. "I have to go now. Grace needs me. Try and remember, okay?"

Try and remember? Try and remember what?

Vivian turned.

"Wait," Addison said. "Please. Don't go. Tell me what I need to remember."

But Vivian kept walking, leaving Addison's mind to run rampant, swirling with unanswered questions. The biggest of them all—whether or not the twins realized they were dead.

CHAPTER 2

Addison jolted up in bed, gripping the bedpost in her hand. Her brow was sweaty, her head throbbing. She glanced over at her boyfriend Luke. He was still sleeping, soundly, like always. A wisp of his blond locks fell over one of his eyelids. She thought about brushing it out of his face, whispering his name, but he looked so peaceful. It didn't feel right to wake him.

She peeled back the covers and slid out of bed, careful to avoid stepping on any squeaky areas on the wood floor while she crossed the hall and entered the bathroom. Mission accomplished, she flicked the switch on the wall, gripped the sides of the countertop with her hands, and glanced at herself in the mirror. Her eyes were bloodshot and puffy, her hair knotty and unkempt, both attributes of an unsettling night's sleep. For a woman of thirty, she looked and felt a hell of a lot older right now.

For a brief moment, her thoughts centered on the dream she'd just had—the manor, the twins. Then it switched to something else—her past. It had been six months since she'd inherited Grayson Manor and moved to Rhinebeck, New York, after her mother's fatal car accident. Six months since she first met Luke. And more importantly, six months since she uncovered the secret about who she *really* was, a medium, just like her mother and grandmother before her.

It was here at Grayson Manor that Addison had encountered her first restless spirit, a deceased actress named Roxanne "Roxy" Rafferty, who went missing in 1952. Thinking back on it now, she recalled the initial terror she felt after waking one night and finding Roxy's spirit hovering at the end of her bed. At the time, she didn't want to believe it was real, didn't want to accept the fact that she'd been given a gift most others didn't possess. She didn't want it—neither the gift nor the responsibility that came with it.

Like it or not, she couldn't ignore it either.

After Roxy's apparition appeared, Addison did some digging into Roxy's past, learned the police suspected she had been murdered. Her body had not been found. Eventually, the case went cold. This explained why Roxy had appeared to Addison in the first place, why she was trapped, and why she'd solicited Addison's help.

Hovering over the bathroom sink now, Addison could almost hear the words her grandmother had spoken to her all those months ago. "Roxy came to you. Only *you* can help her get to where she needs to be."

Had the twins infiltrated her dream for the same reason?

Did they also need her?

CHAPTER 3

"Addison? You there?"

Luke's groggy voice vibrated down the hall. Addison switched the bathroom light off and walked back to the bedroom, stopping when she reached the doorway. Luke was propped up in bed, his back resting on a pillow he'd jammed in front of the headboard. The light from the nightstand cast a fluorescent shadow across his face, and she noticed he was eyeing her strangely.

She half-smiled, tried to pretend nothing was wrong. "I didn't mean to wake you. I was just coming back to bed."

"What time is it?"

"A little after one, I think."

"When did you get up?"

"Five, maybe ten minutes ago."

He tilted his head to the side. "I've been awake for at least twenty."

"I ... ahh ... woke up with a headache and was looking for some ibuprofen in the bathroom."

He tugged at his chin. "Is everything okay?"

"Yeah, why?"

"Your eyes are red. Really red. To be honest, when I first saw you, I thought you'd been crying."

"I haven't. I'm fine."

He stared at her for a moment, didn't speak. He knew something was wrong. He always knew. She walked over, sat down on the bed next to him. He reached out, entwined her hand in his, pulled it to his mouth, and kissed it. "Whatever it is, you know you can tell me."

She smiled. "I know. Do you remember when Roxy first appeared to me?"

He nodded. She continued.

"I think it's happening again."

He leaned back, looked at her like she hadn't said anything out of the ordinary. "I'm not surprised."

"You're not?"

"You knew there would be others. It was the last thing your grandmother told you before she left. Remember?"

"I remember," Addison said. "I guess ... well ... it's just ... it's been several months now, and since it hadn't happened again—"

"You didn't think it would?"

"I don't know what I thought. One day I'm living a normal life, the next a spirit appears to me, and I have to figure out what they want and how to give it to them. It's confusing. I mean, it's not like there's a handbook for dealing with dead people."

"Roxy appeared to you because she couldn't move on until her body was located. Do you think you're dealing with a similar situation?"

"Maybe. I wish I knew how it all worked, how one spirit has the ability to appear to me while millions of others don't. Who decides these things? Someone has to. Even in the afterlife, there has to be a system in place."

He laughed. "A *system?*"

"I'm serious. In my head I picture a giant bowl with all the names of the dead on it, those who haven't crossed over. All the spirits are hovering around it, waiting for their names to be called, like some kind of lottery."

"You can spend your entire life trying to make sense of it, and you never will. Why not focus on what you *can* control, who you can help, how *you* can make a difference?"

Helping Roxy had felt great. It elevated her confidence, gave her a purpose in life, a higher calling. Even so, it hadn't kept the occasional feelings of inadequacy from seeping in, making her feel she wasn't the right person for the job. "What happened tonight, I always assumed it would mimic my first experience. It didn't though. It was different this time."

"Different how?"

"I didn't see anyone. No one appeared to me, I mean. I had a dream. I was standing outside a manor I didn't recognize. There was a tall iron gate. On the right side, in a black metal rectangle, there was a word, or maybe two words partially covered by a tree branch. I made out the first word—Rose—and then the letter C. Nothing else. I assumed it was a family surname. Rosecrest or Rosecrans maybe."

"It's a start. What else did you see?"

"Two young girls. Twins. They were playing together in front of the house. One walked over to me. Her name was Vivian. She said her sister, Grace, wouldn't talk to me because she was afraid."

"Of what?"

Addison shrugged. "I don't know."

"Did she say anything else?"

"She wanted me to remember something."

"Remember what?"

"No clue," Addison said. "She didn't tell me. Everything about the dream was unnatural. The girls were both wearing the same dress. But they were odd."

"The girls?"

"The dresses."

"In what way?"

"They were dated. Thick and plain. Nothing like the clothing girls wear today."

Addison folded a pillow next to Luke's and leaned back. In her dream, the colors were muted and drab, like she was viewing the scene through a filter. The one exception had been the vibrant yellow color of the girls' dresses.

"I just thought of something that seemed insignificant until now," Addison said. "Months ago when we visited Roxy's gravesite, I saw two young girls at the cemetery. They were wearing matching yellow dresses and chasing each other around a headstone. I remember wondering why they weren't with their parents, why they'd been left alone without supervision, and why they were dressed in short sleeves with no jackets during such a cold time of year."

"Did you ever see their parents?"

Addison shook her head. "I watched them for a few minutes. They caught me staring and stopped. One of them waved."

"What did you do?"

"The sun was in my eyes. It was so bright, I could hardly see anything. I closed my eyes. Not for long. A few seconds. When I reopened them, the girls were gone."

Luke squeezed Addison's hand. "I think you just figured out what you were supposed to remember."

CHAPTER 4

Months earlier when Roxy's remains were discovered and she was finally laid to rest at the local cemetery, Addison thought she would visit Roxy's grave on occasion, if for no other reason than to let Roxy know someone was still thinking of her after all these years. She'd never visited though, and she wasn't sure why. Maybe because she no longer felt Roxy's presence like she once did. Roxy never appeared to her again after the night Addison had set her free. She was gone now, and she wasn't ever coming back.

Addison often wondered if that was what happened to spirits after they crossed over. She also wondered whether or not a person could return. She doubted it. Most likely there were higher laws in place, laws governing the living, shielding the dead from the undead, except for the near-death experiences some people claimed to have on occasion.

Still, dead was dead for most people.

Except Addison.

Addison stood in front of Roxy's grave and canvassed the area, trying to recall the exact spot where she'd first seen the twins.

"Anything?" Luke asked.

She shook her head. "It happened so fast, I'm not sure about the exact location now. I thought it would all come back to me once I got here. It isn't."

The truth was, she wasn't sure how to make them reappear again, or if she even could. Twenty minutes passed. No sign of the children.

"What about the general direction of the headstone when you saw the girls?" Luke asked. "Any ideas?"

Addison lifted a finger and pointed, her eyes coming to rest on a tall, column-like monument mounted on four-sided, square pedestals. "I want to say it was somewhere by that obelisk."

They walked together, pausing along the way to read the names on every tombstone they passed. Five rows later, still nothing. No Vivian. No Grace. And no surnames beginning with the word Rose.

"We don't even know if the girls are actually buried here," Addison said. "What if we have it all wrong?"

"What are you suggesting?"

"What if the headstone they were running around belonged to one of their parents instead?"

"Let's say you're right and we should shift our focus, we still don't know what names or dates we're looking for. In your dream, did anything indicate what year it was?"

She considered the question and nodded. "The car."

"What car?"

"Right before I saw the girls, a car drove by. It was an older model Ford. A two-door. If I had to ballpark when it was manufactured, I'd say the mid-seventies."

"Okay, and how old would you say the girls were?"

"Ten or eleven."

He pressed his thumb to his fingers, calculating the results. "I'm only estimating here, but if the girls were eleven in the mid-seventies, their parents might still be alive."

"Then we're missing something. There has to be a connection to this cemetery, a reason they were drawn here."

He frowned. "Wish I knew how to help you."

"This is what Vivian wanted me to remember, Luke. It has to be. There isn't anything else."

Or was she simply wrong about the whole thing?

She was beginning to doubt herself, doubt the dream she had.

"We'll keep looking until we find something." He stepped in front of her, rubbing his hands up and down her arms. "Why don't you try to relax? We're not in a hurry. Close your eyes and let your mind wander. See what happens."

He stepped away, crouching in front of a newer-looking tombstone in the next row.

"What are you doing?" she asked.

"Thought I saw something a second ago."

"What?"

"Can't say for sure. A shiny piece of metal in the grass. Don't see it now though."

He might not, but she did. "It's there, about a foot to your left. See it?"

He swished his fingers along the thick, jade blades of grass, until he clasped the object in his hand. "Huh."

"What is it?"

"A belt buckle on a string. Looks like it slipped off of something, maybe a bouquet on the headstone. When the flowers wilted, it must have slid off."

The buckle was gold plated and rectangular in shape. A brown, circular stone about the size of a quarter was inlaid in the middle. "It must have belonged to the man whose grave this is."

Luke glanced at the headstone. "Cliff Clark. Born May 1945, died December 2014."

"December. Right around the time we were here and I saw the twins." Addison stuck her hand out. "Can I see it?"

Luke placed the buckle in her palm. The moment her fingers grazed its surface, the cemetery swirled around her and everything went black.

CHAPTER 5

The darkness evaporated like a fine mist until the air was clear again. Addison looked around. She was no longer within the safe confines of the cemetery. No longer with Luke. She was in a room, and judging by the rancid combination of bleach and disease streaming through her nostrils, it was a hospital room. She clamped two fingers over her nose, opting to breathe through her mouth until her stomach settled.

It was cold.

Meat-locker cold.

Wherever she was, she wanted out.

The room was dimly lit, the only illumination coming from a dull light bulb screwed into the end of a silver lamp that coiled out several feet from the wall like a detachable hose on a shower faucet. Next to the lamp was a bed, and on top of the bed, a man. He looked old.

Addison guessed somewhere in his upper seventies. His eyes were closed like he was sleeping, even though her instincts told her it wasn't sleep he'd succumbed to.

He was dead.

She didn't know how she knew it.

She just did.

An elderly woman hunched over the side of the bed, weeping, her bowed head twisting left to right. She clasped the deceased man's hand, begging him not to go, not to leave, not yet. His lifeless hand slipped from hers, sagging onto his lap, and she cried out, "Open your eyes, Clifford! Look at me ... please!"

Her pleas had come too late.

Several seconds passed. The woman faded from view like she'd been nothing more than a hologram. Addison's attention was drawn to the other side of the bed, to Vivian and Grace standing side by side, both peering down at the man.

Vivian smoothed a hand across the man's cheek and said, "It's all right, Daddy. It's all over now."

The man's eyes thrust open and he rose up, but his entire body didn't rise with him. His physical body remained still and flat against the bed while his spirit body detached—something Addison had never witnessed before now. He lifted himself into a standing position and glanced back, gazing upon his mortal self for the last time. When he turned around again, he looked different. Younger. Like he'd aged in reverse, his spirit body becoming strong once more, free of the wrinkles that plagued him in his later years. And that wasn't the only change. No longer was he dressed in a paper-thin, dingy, gray hospital gown. He was clothed in white. A shade of white so piercing Addison struggled to gaze upon him without holding out a hand to deflect the blinding rays.

She took a step forward, her eyes fixed on the man who she now recognized. He was the man from her dream. The man behind the wheel of the vintage car.

A beam of light blazed through the open door into the room. The man hesitated for a moment. A look of peace spread across his face, and he smiled. He understood what was coming, what he needed to do next.

Grace yelled, "Daddy!"

The man didn't react, behaving like he didn't notice she was there. She attempted to latch on to the end of his trousers, but Vivian grabbed her from behind, pulling her back.

"No!" Grace yelled. "Daddy, please. Don't leave me, Daddy, stay here! Stay with us! Please!"

He floated toward the light. A moment later, he was gone. Grace sagged to her knees, and Vivian bent down, wrapping her arms around her sister.

"Why did he have to go, Viv?" Grace whimpered. "I thought he was going to be with us now. You *said* he'd be with us."

"He will be, Grace," Vivian replied. "He will be soon. I promise."

"I don't want to be here anymore. I don't like this place."

Vivian extended a hand. "Come on. Let's go home."

The image of the girls faded, and the room disappeared. In a split second Addison found herself back at the cemetery, the belt buckle no longer in her hands. Luke hovered over her.

"What is it?" he asked. "What did you see?"

She steadied her breathing and turned, looking once more at the name on the headstone next to her. "I saw the night Cliff Clark died."

CHAPTER 6

Luke placed a container of Ben & Jerry's Chocolate Therapy ice cream in front of Addison, along with a spoon, and sat across from her at the kitchen table.

"What's this?" Addison asked.

"Ice cream."

Addison peeled off the lid, digging out a hefty scoop. "Yes, but why?"

"Because it's your favorite, and because you need it, and because chocolate fixes everything."

She raised a brow. "Everything?"

"Okay, *almost* everything. You were quiet on the ride home. Do you want to talk about what happened earlier?"

Addison nodded. "The belt buckle must have belonged to the girls' father, Cliff Clark. When I touched it, I found myself inside one of his memories. Well, not one of *his* memories exactly, a memory from the night he died."

It wasn't the first time touching an object had granted her access to a person's past. She'd experienced it before, a few times as a child, and more recently at Grayson Manor. The experiences were always unpredictable, never the same—always leaving Addison with more questions than answers.

"How do you know Cliff Clark is Vivian and Grace's father?" Luke asked.

"They were there, in my vision. Grace called him Daddy."

"The two graves next to Cliff's had the same surname: Clark. They'd been there a lot longer though. I'm guessing they're his parents."

"If the girls' father and grandparents are buried at the local cemetery, there's a good chance the manor is in the area too."

Luke nodded then added, "If the girls are also dead, wouldn't they be buried near their father?"

"Good question. Here's another one. In my vision, I saw Cliff die. I literally watched his spirit body detach from his physical body. Seconds before he crossed over,

Grace tried to get his attention. He didn't seem to hear her. Why didn't he? I mean, if *they're* dead and *he's* dead, why couldn't they communicate with each other?"

Luke tapped a finger on the table, thinking. "He crossed over. They didn't. He was free to move on, and they might be stuck here. Do you have any idea how he died?"

"He was attached to a machine in the hospital room. He was pale, his face an ashy white like he was sick, not just from dying, like he was afflicted or weak with a disease. When I saw him, he was already dead. He'd just passed away."

There were too many questions and too few clues. She needed answers, needed to talk to someone who knew the Clarks' history, someone old enough to tell her what happened to the girls. And she knew the perfect nosey neighbor to ask.

CHAPTER 7

Helen Bouvier coiled her fingers around the curved wood handle of her Birchwood cane and steadied herself. A couple minutes earlier, she'd jerked the living room curtain back a bit too fast and almost toppled over while trying to catch a glimpse of the approaching visitor walking down the dirt road in front of her house. The unwanted distraction, her neighbor Addison Lockhart, was someone she recognized almost immediately. With shoulder-length ginger locks that made Addison's hair look like it was on fire when the sun's rays hit it just right, her young neighbor was impossible to mistake.

The timing of Addison's visit was off.

Way off.

Helen didn't want visitors.

Not now.

The last time they'd seen one another had been a couple of months earlier when Helen popped over to see how Addison was doing. In truth, the inquiry about Addison's welfare was a precursor to the real reason she'd stopped by—to find out if the rumor going around town about Luke taking up residency at Grayson Manor was true.

When he'd answered the door that morning clad in nothing but a pair of boxer shorts and a T-shirt, the answer was obvious. Luke and Addison *were* living together, out of wedlock, no less. And if Luke's not-so-subtle hand grazing across Addison's left butt cheek when he passed her was any indication, they were most likely sharing the same bed too. Probably for quite some time. This revelation didn't bode well with Helen. So when Luke had finally exited the room, she clamped a hand down on Addison's wrist, yanked her to the side, and gave her a good scolding.

Addison had just smiled, and said, "These are different times now, Helen. Thanks for your concern, but I know what I'm doing."

Knew what she was doing?

Women these days.

None of them seemed to have their heads screwed on right anymore.

"How could you *know* anything?" Helen had asked. "Your mother is dead, and your grandmother is off traveling the country. There's no one here to guide you when it comes to these things."

"I don't need a guide. I'm a thirty-year-old woman, not a child."

Thirty.

She'd uttered her age with pride, boasting almost, like she thought thirty was the intellectual equivalent of a woman twice her age. She had no ring on her finger, which meant no commitment. No shock there. Rare was the man who would spring for a ring when the cow *and* its milk came free.

...

The doorbell sounded, a kind of a hollow, repetitive gong that Helen had never grown tired of hearing over the years. The sound always made her feel like she lived in a palace in China, instead of a historical village in New York. She waited several seconds post-gong then shooed her long-time friend Milton toward the door.

Addison rounded the corner seconds later. "It's good to see you again, Helen."

After their last interaction, Helen questioned her sincerity. "You could have called first."

"Why? I knew you were here. You're always home."

"Whether I'm home or whether I'm not is beside the point. Calling ahead is common courtesy."

"I'm sorry. I didn't mean to upset you. I'll call next time. Okay?"

Next time.

"I suppose it doesn't matter now. You're here. Why don't we both have a seat and you can say whatever it is you came to say."

Addison nodded and sat, squeezing her legs and pulling down the hem of her short, bohemian tunic dress to keep from revealing more thigh than she had already.

Helen reached for the tea cup next to her. Intending to put the glass to her lips, she'd lifted it halfway before noticing just how bad her hand was trembling. She set the mug back down.

"Are you, okay?" Addison asked.

"Never you mind. Why did you stop by?"

"Because you're friends with my grandmother."

"*Friends* is a strong word. It would imply I have feelings of affection for Marjorie."

"You *do* have affection for her. You've known each other since you were in your twenties."

Helen didn't understand why Addison was stalling, or why she kept fiddling with the hem on her tunic dress. "What does Marjorie have to do with you being here? Is something wrong? Is she all right?"

"I haven't heard from her in a while. I'm sure she's fine. She always is."

"Then why bring her up at all?"

Addison crossed her arms in front of her. "I was wondering ... it's just ... you seem to know most people in the area, and ..."

"Oh, for goodness sake," Helen said. "Are you going to make your point while I'm still alive to hear it?"

"What do you know about Cliff Clark?"

"It's Clifford," Helen corrected. "Not Cliff."

"Oh...kay. *Clifford* Clark. What can you tell me about him?"

"He's dead. What more is there to say?"

"How did he die?"

"What makes you think *I* know anything?"

The two stared at each other for what seemed to Helen like a ridiculous amount of time. Addison leaned back, the look on her face implying she was satisfied for finally uttering what was on her mind. But what a peculiar thing to ask. Why would Addison be interested in Clifford? He didn't even live in their town, so how did she know him? And why was she prying into his death? It wasn't significant. It was ordinary. Unfortunate, but ordinary nonetheless.

"I can't imagine why Clifford interests you," Helen said. "He didn't live here, in Rhinebeck. As to your question about how he died, I *might* know a few things."

"Such as?"

"Last year, he was diagnosed with coronary heart disease. Nasty business."

"Nasty ... how?"

"The vessels in his body became narrow and hard, making it difficult for blood to get through to the heart. His doctor suggested surgery. Clifford refused at first, until he had a heart attack and his body made the decision for him."

"So, after the heart attack, he agreed to the surgery?"

Helen nodded. "Didn't make things better though. Only made them worse."

"In what way?"

"There were some complications. When the surgeon opened him up, he realized there was significant damage to Clifford's heart tissue. He survived the operation, but his body shut down. He never made it back out of the hospital alive." Helen tipped her head to the side. "Something tells me you already know that part of the story though, don't you?"

"I knew he wasn't alive. I didn't know the specifics of how it happened."

"What else do you know?"

"He had two daughters. They both died when they were young, right?"

There it was, at last. The root. The real reason Addison was sitting in her front parlor querying away. It didn't have to do with Clifford. Not really. It was information on the girls she was after. "Clifford had twin girls. And you're right, they died when they were children."

"How old were they?"

"Around twelve or so, if I remember right." Helen paused. "It was horrible, you know, the way they died. A nightmare no parent should ever have to live through."

"What happened?"

It was so long ago, Helen only recalled vague details. "Seems like it was a holiday. Easter Sunday, I think. The family had gathered together to celebrate at the manor. Aunts, uncles, cousins—all there. After dinner, some of the guests left. Others remained. The children were told to go play in their room so the adults could—"

"When you say *children*, are you referring to the twins, or were other children there too?"

"I can only tell you what was told to me. Nothing more. Now stop interrupting."

Addison's mouth clamped shut. Helen continued.

"The adults were watching television. No. Wait a minute. That's not right. They were having cocktails, listening to music. Yes, yes. It's coming back to me now. When the record finished playing, I believe it was Clifford who got up to change it. He heard a noise outside, a loud thud, followed by another several seconds later. Some of the others heard it too. Rose opened the door, and—"

"Who's Rose?"

Helen frowned at Addison's second infraction.

Addison's hand flew to her mouth. "Sorry. Won't happen again. I promise."

"Rose is Clifford's wife. She opened the door and thought she saw something. She turned on the porch light and walked outside to get a closer look. There, on the cement in their driveway, were the bruised, broken remains of her daughters."

"They were *dead?*"

Helen nodded.

"How?" Addison asked. "I thought you said the children were in their bedroom playing?"

"At some point during the night, they slipped out of their room and crept up to the attic. No one knows why, or how they got inside in the first place. Rose said she always kept the door locked."

"How did they go from playing in the attic to being found dead in front of the house?"

"They fell. When police arrived, they found the window to the attic had been slid open. On the roof was one of Grace's dolls. Since there was no proof of foul play, and no other logical explanation, they speculated both girls attempted to retrieve the doll."

"And they fell in the process."

Helen shrugged. "It's one of those mysteries of life, right along with the deaths of Marilyn Monroe and Natalie Wood. We'll never know for sure."

With no forewarning, Addison bolted from the chair. "I appreciate you taking the time to talk to me."

Helen lifted her cane, preventing Addison from moving forward by prodding her in the thigh with the flat end like she was branding her with it. "Now wait just one minute, dear. Hold on. You're not leaving here until you tell me why you're so interested in the Clarks' story."

"I … ahh … was just curious. I came across something in an old dresser drawer in my house. A newspaper clipping. It mentioned the girls, but didn't say much about how they died. I wondered if you knew the details. That's why I came over."

Helen left the cane where it was, suspicious of Addison's true motives. The gesture seemed to unnerve Addison. She wrapped a hand around the cane in an attempt to remove it, but the moment she touched it, something else happened. Her body went limp and she collapsed on the floor.

CHAPTER 8

"Addison," Helen said. "Addison. Can you hear me? Say something. Speak to me. Hello?"

Addison *could* hear her. She could also feel the palm of Helen's withered hand slapping against the side of her face repeatedly. Her eyes flashed opened. Helen was poised over her, a glass of water in one hand. Milton stood a couple feet away, phone in hand, ready to dial 9-1-1 if need be.

"Were you planning on pouring water on me?" Addison asked.

"If I had to, yes, I was," Helen replied.

Addison sat up. "How long was I out?"

"Not more than a minute. What on earth is going on? Have you ever blacked out before?"

"I … I have to go."

"I think not. You aren't in any position to walk home right now after what just happened. No way. I'll not have it."

Addison boosted herself off the floor, picked her cell phone out of her pocket, and sent Luke a text message. "You know what, Helen? You're right."

"What are you doing? Who are you calling?"

"I'm not *calling* anyone. You don't have to worry. I've asked Luke to come get me."

"You need to sit down, rest for a few minutes."

In the interest of soothing Helen's strained nerves, she complied. She lifted herself back onto the chair and leaned her head to the side, taking a quick glance down the hallway to see if they were alone. "Where did Milton go?"

"I have no idea. Why?"

"How much do you trust him?"

Addison had blurted the question without much forethought as to how her words would be received. Seeing Helen's hand press to her chest accompanied by her stunned expression, she realized she'd been coarse, too coarse, and it was too late to backpedal now.

"What do you mean, how much do I trust him?"

"I only meant, how well do you know him?"

"Don't be absurd," Helen said. "Milton has been my friend and companion for decades. You know this. I trust him with my life. Why would you even ask me such a thing?"

Luke's truck hummed to a stop outside. Addison stood. "I'm sorry, Helen. I don't even know Milton. I'm sure he's very good to you. Forget I asked, okay?"

Addison opened and closed the front door without glancing back, hoping Helen wouldn't follow her out. A vexatious knot burgeoned inside her.

When her hand grazed Helen's cane, she'd caught a glimpse into Helen's future.

A future she wished she hadn't seen.

CHAPTER 9

Addison sat next to Luke atop a white and grey, diamond-patterned wool rug, listening to the wood inside the fireplace crack and whistle. It soothed her somehow, watching the shadowy glow of the flames dance along the adjacent wall. And for a brief moment the worries of her mind faded away, becoming still again.

Luke clutched her hand, caressing her palm with his finger. "What did Helen tell you?"

Addison filled him in on her visit, and what she'd learned about the twins' death. When she finished, he said, "Now we know how they died, but we still don't know where they lived. Did you ask her?"

They actually didn't *know* how they died. What they knew was how everyone else *assumed* they died. "I didn't need to ask Helen where the Clarks lived. I figured it out myself."

"How?"

"We know Cliff was the name of the twins' father. And Helen said their mother's name is Rose. The first part of the sign I saw posted in front of the gate in my dream was *Rose*, only it's not Rosecrest or Rosecrans, it's Rosecliff."

"Their two names together." He bumped shoulders with Addison, grinned. "It's kinda romantic when you think about it. We could put a sign in front of this place one day, change it from Grayson Manor to something else, although AddisonLuke Manor doesn't have the same ring to it."

It was the second time in the last week that he'd mentioned their future. Both times he'd looked her in the eye, gauging her reaction. She'd always been skittish when relationships progressed to this level in the past. It triggered the demons, the failed liaisons, the heartache. A past where kicking things up a notch had always resulted in her getting singed and scarred. Broken. Left to pick up the pieces and start again.

When Luke entered her life, it was like a special kind of oxygen had been pumped into the air. He was different. Honest and pure. Part of her thought she didn't deserve him.

"Hey," Luke said. "Did you hear what I said?"

"About posting a sign with our names on it?"

"I asked if you found anything on Rosecliff when you searched it."

"I did. There's a Rosecliff Manor about twenty miles from here in Pleasant Valley. I thought we could drive over tomorrow. Once I see it, I should be able to tell right away if I'm at the right place."

"And if you are, what then?"

"I hope to make contact with the girls again, see if I can get them to talk to me about what happened the night they died. Thing is, I'm not sure they know they're dead. Vivian might, but I get the impression Grace is confused."

"Any idea how you'll make contact?" Luke asked.

Addison shook her head. "I don't even know if I can get them to appear to me again, but it's worth a try. If they died at the manor, their spirits must still be tied to it."

"What do you think about Helen saying their deaths were considered an accident?"

"How can it be? If Vivian and Grace fell from the window as innocently as everyone believes they did, they should have left this world the moment they died. All these years later, and they're still here. Something's not right."

"They're kids. Maybe they don't know how to get where they're going."

"A small part of me wants to believe they stayed because they didn't want to leave without their parents. I don't think that's how it works though. And even if it was, even if some higher power granted them the choice of whether to stay or go, when I had the vision at the cemetery, Cliff crossed over right after he died. The girls remained here. For whatever reason, they couldn't go with him."

Luke leaned back on his elbows, pressing his hands onto the fibers of carpet. "You said Cliff didn't hear the twins, and he didn't see them, even though they were there in the hospital room with him. It still seems strange to me that they're all dead, the girls could see him, but he couldn't see them."

"I agree. What's even more interesting is how confused Grace was about what was happening. I saw her face when she called out to him. She expected him to answer. Vivian didn't. She made no attempt to keep him here. Her only concern was Grace. She seemed to know they had to stay, and he had to go."

Luke mulled it over in his mind. "Okay, let's say their deaths weren't an accident. What other options are there? What could have happened?"

Addison had been pondering this exact question, trying to recreate the fatal event in her mind. A few things were clear, but so many other things weren't. The kids had been sent away after dinner. They went to the attic. Assuming the attic window was closed at the time, someone opened it. Grace's doll was then tossed onto the roof. After both girls allegedly tried to retrieve it, they fell to their deaths. "There are several gaps I need to fill before I can put it all together. Who opened the window? And why was the doll thrown onto the roof in the first place? Was it a joke, an accident, or was it deliberate and calculated? Was anyone else in the room at the time, and if so, did that person know Grace would go after the doll and in turn, Vivian would go after Grace?"

"Guess we won't know until we dig deeper."

"I'm also curious to know how far away the doll was from the window. Was it close, a foot or two, almost within their grasp, making it more plausible for them to think they could reach it? Or was it deliberately heaved several feet away? If they were around eleven or twelve years old at the time, they were old enough to understand the danger of stepping onto the window ledge to get to the roof. Especially for a doll. Why would they risk it?"

"Vivian could have thrown the doll on the roof and then dared Grace to get it," Luke said. "You said she's been trying to protect her. Have you considered why? Sure, she's her sister, but what if there's more to it? She could be protecting her because she feels guilty about what happened. Think about it."

But they were *both* dead, which meant his theory was wrong.

It had to be.

"I can't imagine Vivian had anything to do with what happened. She was just a child."

Speculation aside, there was one shred of truth to his accusation. If Vivian didn't throw the doll, she might be the only person who knew who did.

CHAPTER 10

The exterior of Rosecliff Manor hadn't altered much over the years. It was like it had been preserved in time, impervious to change. The grass looked the same. The gate looked the same. But the tall, sturdy oak tree towering over the front yard looked different.

Addison pushed the truck door closed and made a beeline for the tree, her eyes focused on the iron fence surrounding it on all four sides. The fence was picket style, with scrolled posts that looked like upside-down hearts.

"The girls were chasing each other around this tree in my dream," Addison said to Luke. "This fence wasn't here though."

She reached the fence, leaned forward, and wrapped her hands around the rails, staring down at a rectangular headstone bearing the words:

IN LOVING MEMORY OF

VIVIAN ASHLEY CLARK AND GRACE ANN CLARK

PASSED AWAY 1ST OF AUGUST 1975

AGED 11 YEARS

REST IN HEAVENLY PEACE

Now Addison understood. The girls weren't buried in the Rhinebeck Cemetery because they were here, at Rosecliff Manor. Why wasn't their father buried here too?

The manor door gust open. A woman in her upper seventies with thin gray hair pinned back into a stiff bun speed-walked toward them. Draped over her white short-sleeved blouse was a black apron with tiny red cherries scattered all over it. A dollop of what appeared to be flour dusted the left side of her cheek. In one hand, she clenched a wooden spoon. The spoon meant business.

At first glance, Addison thought the woman appeared small and frail, with skin so lean and fragile the bones were practically protruding out. What she lacked in size, she made up for with a booming voice that echoed through the air. "You two. Get away from there!"

Addison released her hand from the fence's railing, took a couple steps back. "We were just—"

The woman moved her spoonless hand to her hips. "Who are you? Why are you here?"

Looking to start fresh, Addison stuck out her hand. "You're Rose Clark, aren't you?"

The woman half-closed one eye, retracting away from Addison's hand like it was a snake poised to strike. "How do you know my name?"

Good question. One Addison wasn't ready to answer. Not yet.

"I'm Addison. This is Luke."

"That's *not* what I asked."

"You own Rosecliff Manor, don't you?"

"What about it?"

"I own a manor myself, in Rhinebeck. I was hoping I could talk to you for a few—"

"About what?"

Unsure of how to ease Rose's apprehension, Addison turned to Luke for help.

"I've admired your manor for several years now," he said.

Rose reeled her head around, looking at the manor like she didn't share his fascination. When she turned back, she said, "Why? There are plenty of houses around like this one."

"Not like yours."

"What do you mean?"

"I'm a historical restoration architect," he said. "Every once in a while, I come across a house that stands out the way Rosecliff Manor does. When we drove past, I couldn't help myself. I apologize if we disturbed you. Truth is, we were hoping to get a closer look at the place."

"I ... don't know. I don't know you. Either of you."

Luke dug inside his pocket, pulled out a business card, and offered it to her. "If now's not a good time, I understand. What about another day this week?"

Addison sighed.

Another day this week?

She hoped he hadn't blown their chance to get inside.

"This week?" Rose said. "I'm not sure. I'd have to think about it."

Translation: opportunity over.

A car rounded the corner. Addison squinted in disbelief. It was the vintage Ford she'd seen in her dream. A man sat in the driver's seat. He had a familiar face, but something about him was different than the man who'd been in the driver's seat before. This man was older. He raised a hand, drove in between the manor gates, and pulled to a stop in front of the house.

Rose's expression softened. The man exited the vehicle and walked over, planting a tender kiss on her forehead.

"You didn't tell me you were having anyone over today, Mom," the man said.

Mom?

Helen hadn't mentioned any other siblings.

"I didn't invite anyone over," Rose stated. "These two just showed up."

Dressed in boot-cut jeans and a black pullover sweater, the man looked to be in his mid-fifties. Addison exchanged glances with Luke, certain she knew what was running through his mind—the same thing running through hers. If the man standing next to them was Vivian and Grace's brother, he may have been in the attic the night they died.

The man looked at Luke. "I'm Derek, Rose's son. And you two are?"

"Their names are Luke and Addison," Rose interjected.

"What can we do for you?" Derek asked.

Rose cut in a second time, the wooden spoon in her hand now aimed at Luke. "This one was hoping to see the house." She shifted the spoon to Addison. "And this one appears to be his nosey tag-a-long."

Addison crossed her arms in front of her. "Excuse—"

"I saw the way you were eyeing my daughters' headstone. You wanted a closer look. I bet you would've climbed over the fence and onto their grave if I hadn't stopped ya. *No one* steps over the fence but me. Got it?"

Derek's face reddened. "Why are you interested in my mother's house? It's not for sale."

"No, no," Rose said. "They don't want to buy it. Luke's a restoration something or other. You know, one of those guys who takes an old house and makes it look new again."

Luke peeled off another business card, explaining his job for a second time. Derek listened with interest, then said, "I don't see any reason we can't show them around, Mom."

A still apprehensive Rose frowned. "I ... I don't know. Not today, Derek. Not today. Another day, maybe. We have this young man's card. We can call him later."

The look on her face indicated she had every intention of making sure it was *much* later.

"They're here now," Derek said. "It's not a big deal."

"Thirty minutes?" Luke asked. "And then we'll leave. I promise."

Derek draped an arm around his mother. "Why don't you go back inside, finish cooking, and I'll give these two the grand tour?"

She leaned in like she intended to whisper, but spoke loud enough for everyone to hear. "And you'll stay with them the *entire* time?"

He nodded. "The whole time."

She sighed. "Oh, all right."

Without uttering another word, Rose pivoted on her heel and headed back to the house.

Derek grinned. "So, where are you two from?"

"Rhinebeck," Addison said. "I actually own a manor there."

"Oh, really? Which one?"

"Grayson Manor."

"Huh, I'm not familiar with your place. My father was raised in Rhinebeck, but I haven't spent much time there. Beautiful town."

"If you're ever in the area, feel free to stop by," Addison said. "And I can give *you* the grand tour."

"About my mother ... she's a great person. Really. It's just, we've been through a lot this last year. My dad passed away, and she still hasn't adjusted to life without him."

"Do you have any other siblings?" Addison asked.

"I'm the only one—well, the only one still living, I should say."

"Do you live here with her?"

Derek's head fell back, laughing, like she'd just told a joke. "I don't. I live across town with my wife and our two sons. I look in on Mom three or four times a week. Aside from me, she doesn't really have anyone."

"No friends?"

"Nah, not close ones. Not anymore. She prefers to keep to herself these days."

"I'm sorry about your father."

"Thanks. You know, it's the oddest thing. Some days I still think I'll walk through the front door, and there he'll be, sitting in his favorite recliner in the living room, head buried in a crossword puzzle. Sounds crazy, right?"

Not as crazy as Addison witnessing the man rising from the dead.

"I went through the same thing when my mom died," Addison said. "It wasn't easy to let go."

"But you have ... let go? You found a way to move on?"

"In some ways, I guess. Sometimes I feel her presence, like she's right here, standing beside me."

Derek's attention shifted from Addison to his sisters' headstone. "Yeah, I know what you mean. For a long time as a kid, I thought I could feel my sisters too."

"I noticed they are both buried here, but your father isn't."

"Vivian and Grace died a long time ago. My mother insisted on burying them here because she felt like even though they were dead, it kept them close to her. When they were alive, the three of them used to sit and have a picnic around this tree. Having them here is sentimental, I guess you could say. When Dad died, we talked about the best place for him to be buried and decided it wasn't here."

"Why not?"

"We would have had to take the fence out and move things around. Mom tried to come up with a way to make that happen at first, but she didn't like the idea of doing anything that would disturb her daughters' remains in any way. Besides, Dad wanted to be laid to rest in Rhinebeck."

"Why?"

"Right before my dad's parents died, they purchased a plot for him and my mother right next to theirs. Mom would never agree to be buried there though. She wants to be buried here, at Rosecliff Manor, which would be fine if the estate stays in the family."

"I thought you said she didn't want to do anything to the spot where Vivian and Grace are buried?"

"Well, Mom wants to be cremated, so that's not really an issue."

The keys to the vintage Ford slipped from Derek's hand. Luke bent down, picked them up. "Nice car."

"Yeah, my dad left it to me. Personally, I'd rather be driving my truck any day of the week, but Mom gets a kick out of seeing me in this old thing. I figure if it makes her happy, it's the least I can do. So ... you two ready to see the house?"

CHAPTER 11

Finding the right opportunity to slip away once inside Rosecliff Manor proved more difficult than Addison imagined. Every room they entered, Derek followed behind, always lingering in doorways, blocking her from stepping out, doing any exploring on her own. His intentions seemed more innocent than contrived. But were they?

After a tour of two bedrooms on the second level of the house, they passed a stairway so narrow one would almost have to turn sideways to climb its steps. Addison stopped, hoping Derek would pick up on her interest and follow suit. Instead, he passed the stairwell like it didn't exist, continuing on to the next room without uttering a word.

Addison remained. "What's up there?"

Derek didn't look back. "Oh, nothing."

"There's a stairway here. Doesn't it go to something?"

"An attic. We don't use it."

"Not even for storage?"

"It's empty for the most part. I couldn't say for sure. I haven't been inside the attic for ages."

"I'd love to see it."

Her persistence finally paid off. He reeled around, eyeing her like she'd become a nuisance. "You can't. Thing is, I couldn't even show it to you if I wanted to."

"Why not?"

"It's locked."

"Doesn't your mother have a key?"

"She lost it a long time ago."

"And she never had another one made?"

He shook his head. "Don't think so."

"Are you sure it's even locked?" She thumbed upstairs. "I could run up, jiggle the handle a few times, see what happens. In old houses like this, you never know—I might get lucky."

Derek crossed his arms, leaned against the wall. "Why is it so important to you? Isn't Luke the restoration guy? I mean, why do I get the feeling you'd do just about anything to go up there?"

Fumbling over her words she replied, "You see, we, umm ..."

Derek put up a hand, stopping her. "I see what's going on here."

"You do?"

"Don't say another word. Not out here."

He turned, signaling to Addison and Luke to follow him. They walked into a long, rectangular library. A formal sitting area with a black velvet sofa and two chairs rested over a colorful oriental rug in the room's center. Vintage books, the kind only seen in antiquarian bookshops, lined the floor-to-ceiling, mahogany-stained shelves on all four walls.

Once inside, Derek closed the door. Voice lowered, he directed his attention back to Addison. "Do you know how my sisters died? I mean, you obviously do."

"I've heard things."

"What *things?*"

"I was told what happened was an accident."

Addison stared at Derek, hoping to gain some insight into what he might be thinking. But his expression was blank and opaque, giving away nothing.

"Are you a reporter?" he asked.

"No."

"Writing a book?"

"No."

"You're not?"

"No, I'm not. Neither one of us are."

"Why should I believe you?"

His tone had changed. It was no longer playful and relaxed. It was terse. Apprehensive. Whatever trust he may have felt before had obviously vanished.

"Aside from my curiosity about the attic, I haven't asked anything," Addison said. "If I was a reporter, wouldn't I ask more questions?"

"Maybe you would, maybe you wouldn't. *Maybe* you were trying to butter me up before you tightened the screws, admitted what you're really after."

"What is it you think we're after?" Luke asked.

"How are you two affiliated with Thomas Gregory?"

In unison Luke and Addison both said, "Who?"

"Tom Gregory. He's a wannabe writer whose books never sold. A few years ago when his books weren't selling, he went another route and put together a historical picture book on some of the older houses in the area, those more than a hundred years old. He included Rosecliff."

"You mean to say your parents aren't the original owners of this place?" Luke asked.

"They didn't inherit it, no. My parents purchased the manor a few years after I was born. At that time, it was in desperate need of repair, which, as you've seen, they spent a lot of money doing. In Tom's narrative, he discussed the night of my sisters' deaths in detail, which was bad enough. But he didn't stop there. He put a permanent stain on our family by alleging the police didn't conduct a thorough investigation after they died."

"Based on what?"

"In his opinion, not enough evidence was collected to prove their deaths were accidental."

Addison did her best to remain impartial about the information Derek was sharing, hoping if she remained calm, he'd keep feeding her more. "How would Tom know if the investigation was done right? What makes him an expert?"

Derek shook his head. "I don't know. I've asked myself the same question a hundred times. I looked into him. He wasn't even alive when it happened. For whatever reason, he made the decision to dredge up the past and attack my family."

"Do you know anything about him or his background?"

"Aside from his age and what he does for a living, I can't find jack shit on this guy."

"Has anything ever come up over the years to suggest his opinions are valid?"

"His opinions *aren't* valid. How could they be? When I asked around town, I found out he was a washed-up science fiction author. Washed-up meaning he wrote two novels that didn't sell."

"How did he go from a fiction author to publishing a non-fiction picture book?"

"Who knows? All I know is, when the book first came out, it received plenty of attention locally. I'm guessing that's what he was after. Why else would he perpetuate such lies?"

"You're right. It doesn't make much sense."

"Once news got around about it, seemed like every person in town bought a copy. There was a kind of renewed interest in what happened, almost cult-like. I caught a few people pulled to the side of the road in front of Mom's house, pointing at the attic window, and taking pictures. It hasn't been easy, especially for my mother, to have this all dragged up again. When she saw you on the property today, I'm sure she thought you were here because of what you read in the book."

"I suppose there wasn't much you could do once the book was released, but did you ever consider talking to Tom, telling him your side of the story? I mean, I assume you were here the night your sisters died."

It was the "in" Addison had been waiting for, the one she hoped would shed new light on what happened to Vivian and Grace. Instead, Derek became silent. It was like he'd gone numb, like he was somewhere else, back in time perhaps, recalling the events in his mind.

"Derek," Addison asked. "Are you okay?"

His eyes widened, snapping him back into the here and now. "No. No, I'm not."

CHAPTER 12

"You all about done up there?" Rose yelled. "Thirty minutes passed thirty minutes ago."

Derek hollered, "It's not their fault, Mother. It's mine. We'll be down in a few minutes."

"Thanks for taking time to show us around," Luke said. "I mean it. This place is amazing. We can't thank you enough."

"Hey, look. I'm sorry I accused you two of anything. It's just been hard, you know?"

"There's no need to apologize. Sounds like your family has been through a lot lately. You have every right to be on edge."

Although the visit wasn't a complete loss, it was far from what Addison had envisioned. With no sign of the girls and no way of getting into the attic, she felt like she'd failed—not only herself, but also the girls.

Derek stood. "Hey, I almost forgot. There's an old homestead house out back. More of a storage shack, really. It was already here when my parents bought the place. Used to play in there as a kid. It's so old it has a historical plaque on the front. Thought you might be interested in taking a look at it before you leave."

Luke nodded. "Absolutely."

Out of the corner of her eye, Addison caught a faintest glimpse of white. "Do you mind if I use the restroom first and meet you two at the homestead when I'm done?"

Derek considered the request. "I ... guess so. I tell you what, we'll head out back. I suggest you steer clear of my mother. It's best not to let my mother know you're in here without me."

"Absolutely. I wouldn't want to get you in any trouble."

Derek cracked a smile. "I'm concerned for your sake, not mine."

He and Luke left the room. Once they were out of sight, Addison glanced over the sofa, seeing what she thought she had before. "Shadow? Where did you come from?"

She bent down, reaching a hand toward the cat. The cat jerked away. Addison retracted her hand. "All right, all right. I get it. You don't want me to pick you up."

Shadow crossed the room, stopping in front of one of the bookshelves. He looked at the books then back at her, almost like he was trying to tell her something. While she pondered the unlikely possibility, Shadow rubbed his head across the spine of a few books on the bottom shelf.

"What are you doing, you crazy cat?"

Shadow responded by ramming the top of his head against the same set of books a second time. They slid back, and Addison heard a tinging noise which couldn't have come from one of the books. She walked over and knelt down. Shadow scurried out of the room.

Reaching back, she felt behind the books, and her hand came to rest on something thin, cold, and hard. She fisted her hand around the object and pulled it toward her, surprised when her eyes came to rest on a long brass key.

Footsteps approached.

"What are you doing in here? Where's my son?"

Addison looked over at Rose. Hands on hips, Rose stamped a foot on the ground, waiting for an answer.

Addison closed her hand around the key again, slipping it inside her back pocket. "I was admiring your library."

"*Where's* my son?"

"He's showing Luke the homestead house. I hear it's quite old."

"Why aren't you with them? You were supposed to stay together. He told me you'd all stay together. This isn't a museum or an exhibit on display. It's my house."

"I was with them," Addison lied. "When I was in the library earlier, I was so intrigued by all of your books, I wandered back here while they were talking. I doubt Derek saw me leave. Please, don't blame him. Blame me."

The sincerity in Addison's voice seemed to win Rose over. For now.

"I suppose I can't blame you for wanting to spend some time in here. It's my favorite room in the house."

Addison spread her hands to the side. "This room is amazing. You must have over five hundred books."

"Over a thousand, actually."

"Which one is your favorite?"

"Asking me which is my favorite is like asking me which of my three children is my favorite. All of them."

"Oh, I should tell you Shadow was in here a few minutes ago. I tried picking him up, but he ran out."

Rose's complexion paled. "What did you just say? How did you know Shadow's name? I never mentioned him to you."

In an attempt to repair the damage, Addison said, "Your son must have said something to me."

"Why would he?"

"Why wouldn't he? Shadow is your cat, isn't he?"

"*Was* my cat. Shadow's dead."

CHAPTER 13

Derek stood on the front porch steps, his hands shoved halfway inside the back of his pant pockets. He watched Addison hoist herself into the truck, watched Luke rev the engine a couple times before steering the vehicle onto the road and driving away. They seemed like decent people, but thinking back on the previous hour he'd spent with them, he believed his mother had been right to express initial concern. They were meddlesome. And though Luke's knowledge of the manor couldn't be refuted, his self-proclaimed affection for the place seemed like a lot more than admiration alone.

Then there was his sidekick, Addison, a woman whose keen interest wasn't centered on the house itself. He'd kept a sharp eye on her during the tour, noticing the way her eyes darted around, never pausing long enough to focus on any one thing. He wondered about the real reason she'd asked to use the restroom.

Rose placed a hand on his shoulder. "She knew Shadow's name. Do you really expect me to believe you just happened to mention him to her? You hated that cat as a boy. You teased it relentlessly."

"I didn't *hate* the cat. I've never cared for cats. I'm a dog person."

"Exactly my point. Why mention the cat at all?"

Derek stepped back inside the house, closed the door, and turned. "You worry too much."

She was right to worry, of course, and to express her uncertainty. He'd lied when questioned about the fur ball minutes ago. Even now, he wasn't sure why he'd done it. Better to corroborate Addison's story for now than admit his instincts about her may have been wrong. His mother had enough to worry about. Still, there were questions he needed answers to.

How *had* she known the cat's name?

And even stranger—how the hell did she think she saw the cat alive and in the library?

CHAPTER 14

Thomas Gregory was an easy man to find. Almost too easy. After a quick pit stop at one of the few bookstores in town, not only did a female store employee offer precise directions to his place, she also wrote his physical address on a piece of paper, folded it, and offered it to Luke along with a wink and smile.

So much for privacy.

Or hiding one's motives.

When Luke unfolded the bit of crumpled paper, he was startled to find the unexpected freebie that came along with it—the female employee's own phone number scribbled beneath Tom's address. Luke shook his head then laughed, acknowledging the girl in a polite "thank you but no thank you" tone of voice. He then draped an arm around Addison and walked outside, tossing the note into a trash receptacle behind him.

CHAPTER 15

In the time it took Luke and Addison to drive to Tom's place, Addison had read through the chapter Thomas devoted to Rosecliff Manor in his book *Pleasant Valley: A History in Pictures.* In the chapter, he accused police officers of several things—shoddy detective work, failure to thoroughly interview all witnesses, and Addison's personal favorite, failing to figure out the true motive of the crime. His words were baseless and presented with an overabundance of bias, almost like the claims he made were accompanied by a personal agenda.

Tom's house, if one considered a fifth-wheel trailer popping a squat on an otherwise vacant property a house, was located on a ten-acre parcel of land with no other dwellings around it. Halfway to the trailer, a man Addison assumed was Tom stepped out of an open door, sitting on one of the metal, fold-down steps in front of him. Steaming cup of coffee in hand, he watched and waited as they approached.

Tom was nothing like Addison imagined, his look more tree-hugging hippie than non-fiction book author. Dressed in a pair of light blue, relaxed-fit jeans, a gray crew neck T-shirt, and Teva sandals, he was young. Late twenties in her estimation. He wore a pair of oval-shaped, rimless glasses over his eyes, and had long, straight brown hair bundled into a loose ponytail behind his neck.

Luke spoke first. "Thomas Gregory?"

The man took a few swallows of coffee and leaned back, resting his elbows on the vinyl floor just inside the camper's entrance. "It's Tom. Who's askin'?"

"My name's Luke, and this is Addison. We heard you wrote a book on some of the historical homes in the area."

"I did. What about it?"

"You made some interesting assumptions about the Clark girls, Vivian and Grace."

Tom lowered his head, making a face like he'd grown weary of the topic. "I'll tell you what I tell everyone else. I don't regret what I wrote in the book. I gave my honest opinion, and I stand by it. It's called freedom of speech, dude, and this is a free country. Too bad if people don't like it."

"An opinion isn't the same thing as proof," Luke said.

"I know it isn't. That's why I stated it was my opinion and mine alone. Didn't matter though. They all flipped out over it."

"Who did, the Clark family?"

Thomas swished a hand through the air. "Nah. The Clarks never bothered me. Have to say, I was surprised they didn't. I mean, it's a small town. I heard they were angry."

"If not them then who?"

"All the old-timers around here—the ones who were alive when it happened. Most of 'em accused me of being a failed author who only wrote the book to make a quick buck."

Or to garner attention, as Derek had blamed him for earlier.

"*Are you* trying to make a quick buck?"

Thomas eyed Luke for a moment then extended his arm to the side, grunting out a laugh. "You can see how rich it made me. If it was money I was after, I wouldn't have written a book about a place only the people who live in it care about."

Looking at Tom now, Addison had no reason not to believe him. His jeans were clean, but ripped in three places. Not in a fashionable way—in an old, worn-out way. The mug he drank from had a small chip around the base. It looked cheap. Thrift store cheap.

He wasn't showy, and he wasn't vain. Still, there was more to it than one man's opinion. There was motive. She just needed to find it.

"If you didn't write it for the money, why write it at all?" Addison asked. "You could have included a few photos of the house and omitted the rest. You didn't."

"If you're trying to accuse me of—"

"We're not here to accuse you of anything. We have our own suspicions about what happened to the Clark girls, and they have nothing to do with what you said or didn't say. We're after the truth."

Tom raised a brow, taken aback by her statement. "Really? Why?"

"Our interest in the details of what happened is genuine."

"She's telling the truth," Luke said.

"If it's such a big deal to you, why don't you do your own digging?" Thomas asked.

"We are, and we have been," Addison said. "Rose Clark and her son Derek didn't have much to say."

"You talked to the Clarks?"

"Didn't you?"

"I tried. Once. I drove to the house. Rose opened the door. I told her I was writing the book and what I planned to say. I said if she had anything to say on the subject, I'd like to hear it. She slammed the door in my face."

"You saw the police report, right? That's what you said in the book."

He nodded. Addison continued.

"Would you mind if we sat down, asked you some questions about what was in it?"

Thomas glanced back, then looked at Addison and said, "I'd invite you inside, but my humble abode is a mess right now."

Except, it wasn't a mess at all.

From her vantage point, Addison had a clear view of the front half of the trailer. It was pristine. No dishes in the sink, nothing left out on the counter, and no décor to speak of except for a small, wallet-sized picture of a woman in a wooden frame sitting on the windowsill. When he'd turned back a moment earlier, the photo seemed to catch his attention.

Questions filled Addison's mind.

Who was the woman in the photo?

Why did Tom say his trailer was dirty when it wasn't?

What was he hiding?

Her gaze lingered on the picture long enough for Tom's apprehension to kick in. He hopped off the trailer steps, closing the door behind him. Motioning to a wood, chipped, sun-damaged picnic table several feet away, he said, "Let's sit here."

They sat.

"Why are you interested in the Clark girls?" Tom asked. "Idle curiosity? You read the book and now you want more details? If so, I'm not your guy."

Addison shook her head.

"What then?"

"It's personal."

"Personal, how?" Tom asked. "Are you related?"

"I can't say."

"Why not?"

She'd have to do better if she expected him to open up. "I may be able to find out the truth about what happened the night they died. The real truth. I don't know how much it matters to you, but it matters to me."

He set the coffee cup down. "I wouldn't have taken the time to write about it if it didn't."

"And I wouldn't have taken the time to come here today if it didn't mean something to me. So help us. Please."

He crossed his arms, resting them on the edge of the table. "What do you want to know?"

"You saw a copy of the police report, but some of the things you said in your book aren't found in a standard police report. Where did you get your information?"

"I have a source."

"What source?"

"Can't say."

"Why not?"

"I don't want to get anyone in trouble," he said.

"Were you even telling the truth when you said you actually looked at a copy of the report?"

"There's a waiting period. You just don't go in, get a report handed to you right away. Sometimes it takes days. And even then, you're only viewing a copy. Who knows what they leave out of those things? A little whiteout, and a person wouldn't even know what they're missing."

"Are you're trying to say you viewed the *real* report, not a copy?"

He rubbed a hand across the back of his neck. "I'm not *saying* anything. And, just so you know, if any part of this conversation gets around, I'll deny it. All of it."

"I get it."

"Oh, you do, do you?"

"We just met. You don't have any reason to trust us."

"You're right," he said. "I don't."

"Trust goes both ways."

"No, it doesn't. It goes *one* way. I'm not trying to gain your trust. Look, the two of you seem nice enough. You have to understand, there are things I can't say, things I don't have any right talking about, things told to me in confidence."

"Is there anything you *can* tell us?"

He paused, thought it over. "Okay, I'll say this. I ordered a copy of the police report to cover my ass. I knew once the book came out, there'd have to be a paper trail proving I actually ordered the report in order to make what I said legitimate. But let's just say it may not have been the only information I received."

It wasn't a lot to go on, but it was a start.

"I still don't see why the Clarks' story interests you."

"You and me, we're not the only people trying to find out what really happened the night those girls died. They may be gone, but not everyone has forgotten."

There *was* someone else, someone using Tom to stir up conversation again. Although small, the portrait of the woman in Tom's window was familiar. Too familiar. "What makes you think Vivian and Grace died under mysterious circumstances?"

"For starters, you have to consider what investigations were like back then. Grace and Vivian died in the mid-seventies. Forensics was limited. We're talking Polaroid pictures. AFIS wasn't in place yet. There were no camcorders, no light sources capable of detecting things like fibers or body fluids, things not visible to the naked eye. No DNA fingerprinting. The list goes on."

"Even if they had better technology at the time, there's still no proof the girls' death wasn't accidental," Addison said.

"Oh no? The police report stated they found a doll on the roof of the house. You could say it was the doll that led police to believe the girls fell while trying to retrieve it. It's the only logical explanation, right? I mean, it's not like they were up there daring each other to jump out of a third-story window."

"What's your point?"

"Wouldn't it be interesting to process the evidence again? The doll, the attic, what the girls were wearing that night?"

"You really think they'd find anything in the attic after all this time?"

"Rose has a neighbor who's lived in the neighborhood since 1973. According to her, once police closed the case, Rose locked the attic and never allowed anyone in there again. If she's right, it's been preserved in time. I mean, I'm no DNA expert, but it makes you wonder, doesn't it? On the night of the party, no one admitted to being in the attic. Everyone said the girls must have been in there alone. Know what I think? Someone is lying."

CHAPTER 16

Luke slid open the top drawer of the dresser, pulled out a tiny square box and propped it open, staring down at the lustrous, circular-shaped jewel centered on top of a platinum wedding band. A smile spread across his face as he thought about how disheveled Addison had looked the day they met, when she hired him to do the restoration work on Grayson Manor. She was so fragile then, so adrift after losing her mother. Bright-eyed and with an innocent charm she wasn't even aware she possessed, no woman had ever made such an intense first impression on him.

Up to then, he'd led a good life, a content life. He was a bachelor and proud of it. He'd reworked every square inch of the historic one-bedroom house he purchased in his twenties until it looked brand new again, even better than the original.

Over the years, he'd had several relationships, a couple of them serious, lasting more than a year. None proved strong enough to span the test of time. They were all decent women. Kind women. Any one of them would have made a good choice for a lifelong companion. Just not a great one. In every one of those relationships there was always something missing, something holding him back from reaching the point of a proposal.

Until now.

Until Addison.

They hadn't even been together a year, in fact, they'd only known each other for a few weeks before he looked in her eyes one day and realized there was no question about where his future would lead. No question about who he'd share the journey with. Now, he couldn't imagine a single day without her in it.

The night before, his proposal was all planned out. Where he'd do it. How he'd do it. It had festered in his mind for weeks until it was only one night away, and then the craziness started. And somehow now it didn't seem fair. Not to her. Not to the twins. Her mind was clouded now. Occupied. Unable to process the one thing he thought would make him burst if he couldn't tell her.

He gazed on the ring one last time, snapped the ring box closed, and concealed it beneath layers of folded T-shirts.

It could wait.

And he could wait.

Even if he couldn't, he had to.

CHAPTER 17

At exactly one o'clock in the morning, Luke's snoring gave Addison the green light she'd been waiting over two hours for. He was asleep. Time to put her plan into action. Part of her hesitated for a brief moment. She regretted sneaking out of the house this late at night without telling him. It almost felt like a betrayal, like she was going behind his back, even though she wasn't. Or maybe she was. Either way, her intentions were good. She meant well. She knew what had to be done, knew the potential danger. She also knew it was something she'd be glad she did alone if it all went wrong.

The tires on Addison's car crunched along the dirt driveway until she made it onto the road, her eyes still fixed on the second-story window of the room she'd walked out of not two minutes before. The lights were still off. He was still asleep. A positive sign.

Twenty-nine minutes later she flicked the car's headlamps off, inching to a stop in front of a vacant lot next to Rosecliff Manor. She ducked between two bowed iron rods in the gate, slid through, and made her way to the back of the house. Twisting the mini-flashlight to "on," she beamed the tiny light across the yard, scanning the area. Earlier she'd spotted a ladder leaning next to the shed out back. It was long enough for her to climb to the second-story window, the same window she'd managed to crack open when no one was looking during the tour earlier.

Ladder in hand, she lined it up with the window and began her ascent. With Rose's bedroom located on the main floor and the attic on the third, she could only pray she could get in and out without arousing suspicion. Four steps up, the flashlight slipped from her hand, clanking on one of the ladder's steps before breaking apart on the ground. Addison froze. How far had the sound traveled? Far enough to wake a neighbor? Far enough to wake up Rose?

Several minutes passed in silence, the only source of light coming from a partially clouded moon. She took a step, then another. She reached the top, slid open the window, and climbed inside. Flattening her body against the wall, she inched her way to the room's edge. She rounded the corner and began her second climb of the night, this time on the narrow steps leading to the attic.

The attic door felt as solid as it was wide. Using the tip of her finger to find the keyhole, she dug her other hand inside her pocket, slid the key all the way inside the hole, and turned it. The lock didn't click, but when she pressed forward, the door cracked open, filtering a musty combination of dust and grime. She pressed her nose to the sleeve of her jacket to quench the desire to gag.

She reached out a hand, feeling her way along the wall for a light switch. There wasn't one, and without her flashlight to guide her, she had little choice.

In a hush, she said, "Vivian, if you're here, show yourself. Please."

Silence.

"Vivian, please. I'm here to help. I remember now."

A delicate child's voice answered, "Do you know how to help us?"

The voice was Vivian's.

"I'd like to try," Addison said. "I need to talk to you and your sister about what happened the night of your parents' party."

"Close the curtains."

To Addison, it seemed a far-out request. "What?"

"Close the curtains so no one can see inside."

"I can't. I don't know where they are."

"Straight in front of you. Walk slow. You'll get there."

Addison took several steps forward. She reached the other side of the room and waved a hand across the air until the she felt the cold, hard glass in front of her. She stretched both arms out to the side, curled the edges of the pleated cotton fabric in her fist, and drew the curtains closed.

She turned.

A faint orb of light illuminated the room, soft and dull at first. An image shaped to life a few feet from where she stood.

Vivian looked at Addison then turned, her eyes coming to rest on a coat closet. "It's okay. You can come out. We talked about this. You know it's what we have to do now."

"Is ... Grace inside the closet?" Addison asked.

Vivian nodded. "I thought she'd come out this time, but she won't."

"Can I try?"

Vivian shrugged. "Guess so."

Addison bent down in front of the closet door but didn't open it. "Grace, if you can hear me, please know you don't have to be afraid. It's okay. I want to help you. You and Vivian both."

No reply.

"I'm going to open the door to the closet and back away," Addison said. "You come out whenever you're ready."

Addison grasped the round, wooden knob in her hand and tugged the door back, waiting until it was three quarters of the way open before she peeked around the door's corner. "She's not here. Where did she go?"

Vivian shrugged. "She disappears sometimes. She's probably somewhere in the house. Maybe with Mama. She likes to watch her when she sleeps."

Addison knelt in front of Vivian. "Do you know why you're here?"

"Do you mean, do I know I'm dead?"

Addison nodded.

"Yes. I know."

"Does Grace know?"

"I think so. She doesn't like to talk about the night we died."

"Because of what happened?" Addison asked. "What *really* happened?"

Vivian nodded. "And because Grace is scared to leave. She won't, so we're stuck here."

"Could *you* move on if you wanted to, without Grace?"

"I don't know. I haven't tried. Even if I could, I'd never leave her here alone."

"You're a good sister, Vivian."

Vivian tilted her head to the side. "How can you see us? No one else can."

"When I was a little girl, younger than you, I received a gift."

"A present?"

"No, not the kind you open. It lets me see people like you even though you're not alive anymore."

"How?"

"I'm not sure how it happens. I just know I see the people I'm supposed to see when I'm supposed to see them. In my family, the gift passes down from mother to daughter when we're five. Only, my mother didn't use her gift, and when it passed to me, she didn't want me to use mine either."

"Why not?"

"She had a bad experience as a child. She didn't understand she could help people trying to move on from this life to the next."

"Like the woman in the pink dress? The one buried in the cemetery?"

Addison raised a brow, surprised. "Like her, yes. How do you know about Roxy?"

"She waved at me. She said you were a nice lady and not to be afraid to talk to you because you could help me."

Two thoughts occurred to Addison simultaneously. First, the day she saw Vivian and Grace at the cemetery, Vivian might not have been waving at her but at Roxy. Second, maybe that's how it worked. After one person moved on, they chose who she helped next. "Vivian, what do you remember about the night you died, about when you and Grace were playing in the attic?"

"It's hard for me."

"What's hard?"

"Remembering."

"Why?" Addison asked.

"The longer we're here, the more I forget."

"I need you to try for me. Okay?"

Vivian nodded. Addison continued.

"On the night of your parents' party, you were sent away after dinner. Then what happened?"

"Grace heard someone in the attic, and Mama said no one was allowed in there without her permission."

"Why not?"

"It's where she kept all the special stuff. The things she didn't want us to play with."

"So the two of you decided to go to the attic and check it out."

"Uh-huh."

"Who did you see when you got up there?"

"Boys."

"What boys?"

"I don't know. Their faces are blurry now. I try to see them sometimes, try to remember, and I can't."

Had Vivian blocked out all of her memories because they were too painful to see?

"Can you remember how many boys were in the attic?" Addison asked.

"Two. Wait, three. I think."

"Were they your age—older, younger?"

"They were ... taller than me, I think."

"So they were older. How much older?"

"I don't know."

"Who opened the attic window?"

"I did."

"Why?"

"It was hot. We were sweaty from playing the game."

"What game?"

"Hide-and-seek."

Addison glanced around the room, noting the size. It was equivalent to a classroom in an elementary school. And sparse. With the exception of the coat closet, only a few boxes of toys remained. None big enough to hide inside. "There aren't a lot of places to hide in here."

"It used to be filled with stuff. Mama took it all out."

"When you were playing, who took Grace's doll and threw it onto the roof?"

Vivian's face scrunched up, and she uttered two words that would change everything. "What doll?"

CHAPTER 18

Was it possible Vivian was lying about the doll? No. She couldn't be. Looking at her now, the child appeared flummoxed by Addison's question. And yet, there *had* been a doll, a doll that was the core everything. Every clue, every suspicion, every conclusion.

If the doll had nothing to do with their deaths, what did? Or who?

"Vivian," Addison began, "the police found a doll on the roof the night you died."

"Well, I didn't put it there."

"I believe you, but someone did. The police decided you and Grace fell from the attic window after trying to retrieve the doll from the roof."

"What does *retrieve* mean?"

"It means trying to get something."

"Grace wouldn't ever go on the roof. She wouldn't even climb trees with me."

"Who else knew this about her?" Addison asked.

"I don't know. Just me, I guess."

"Are you saying your parents didn't know? Or your brother?"

"I don't know. Maybe."

"Did you play with dolls? Did Grace?"

"Nah. Mama bought them for us, but we liked other things, like Mr. Potato Head. Did your mom buy you a Mr. Potato Head?"

Addison didn't hear the question. Her mind was elsewhere, processing what Vivian had told her so far. A doll was found on the roof, except Vivian had no recollection of it. Grace was afraid of heights. Neither of the girls liked dolls, so it was unlikely either of them would have cared enough to go after it.

"Vivian, do you have any idea how you died?"

"I see pictures in my head sometimes. They're really fuzzy, like when we used to drive in the car real fast on the freeway and I looked out the window at all the trees."

If Addison was going to get to the truth, she needed to jog Vivian's memory. "I'm going to try something, and I don't want you to be afraid, okay?"

Vivian nodded. "Okay."

Addison walked to the attic window, brushing one curtain panel to the side with a hand. She felt a sharp pain and looked down. Her finger was bleeding, having been cut on a sliver of wood next to a bent, rusty nail jutting out from the corner of the windowsill.

"What are you doing? Don't open the curtains. Someone might see!"

"It's okay. I have to do this, Vivian. Trust me."

Addison closed her eyes and pressed both hands onto the window ledge. When her eyes opened, the room had changed. The attic was no longer bleak and depleted in contents. It was filled to the brim with furniture and boxes, all sorts of play toys and unwanted items. Music boomed through the house, the tune a familiar one—something her own mother played when she was a child. "Jive Talkin'" by the Bee Gees. The sound permeated every orifice, drowning out everything else in its wake.

A pig-tailed girl in a yellow dress faced the corner, counting. "Seventeen, eighteen, nineteen, twenty."

The girl turned, hands on hips, sizing up the room like a predator stalking its prey. The girl was Grace or Vivian, but Addison couldn't determine which.

The girl said, "Ready or not, here I come."

She tore through the room, yanking lids off boxes, opening dresser drawers, glancing behind a piano, an old wooden bed frame, a mirror. Seconds later she clapped her hands. "You're busted, Viv! I got you! Boo-yah!"

Vivian's head poked out from behind a painting of a fruit bowl slanted against the wall. "Take a chill pill, Grace. It's just a stupid game. Don't be such a cheese weasel."

"Yeah, but I gotcha. You're it!" Grace's exuberance changed when her attention deviated to an object in Vivian's hand. "What's that?"

Vivian flattened one hand over the other, concealing the item between them. "What's what?"

"What you're holding in your hand. What is it?"

Vivian jerked her hand behind her back. "It's nothin'. Don't worry about it."

"I'm not *worried.* Tell me what it is."

A boy popped out of a cardboard box a couple feet in front of Vivian. At least, Addison assumed he was a boy. He had light brown hair, parted in the center with layered, backward-facing curls framing his face. His long, feathered bangs fell over his eyes, making it impossible for Addison to get a good look at him. He patted down his back pockets, stuck out a hand, and said, "Hey, that's mine. Give it back!"

"Give *what* back?" Vivian sneered. "*Thisss?*"

"You shouldn't have ... you shouldn't have taken it. It's not yours."

"I didn't *take* anything. You dropped it when you were hiding. I picked it up. Finders keepers."

"It's ... that's ... not for you. Don't open it."

Vivian's shoulders bobbed up and down. "Too late. Already did."

The boy's face reddened. "I'm not playing anymore, Viv. Give it back. Now. Stop horsing around."

Vivian giggled, whinnied, and galloped to the other side of the room. The boy followed. Addison looked on, hoping to catch enough of a glimpse of the boy's face to determine he was Derek. Vivian was right. He *was* taller, and older than the girls by a few years or more. His high-pitched voice indicated he hadn't matured yet.

Vivian stuck a hand out the attic window, dangling the item between two fingers. "You want it? Come and get it!"

"Stop it," the boy said. "It's not funny."

Vivian lowered her hand so it couldn't be seen, looked at the boy and said, "Oopsies."

The boy raced to the window, a look of relief on his face when she lifted what appeared to be folded paper over her head and said, "Psyche!"

"Give it, Viv. Give it here!"

The boy's tone had changed. It was different now. Hard. Demanding. And something more.

Furious.

Vivian gripped the paper, waving it over her head. The boy careened into her and reached out, snatching the paper away at last and shoving into his back pocket. The weight of his body too heavy to sustain, Vivian stumbled back, her hand grasping for the wall as her body fell out the window. She started to say, "Help!" but it was too late. She slid out the window and was gone.

The boy backed away, his eyes wide with disbelief.

Grace ran to the window and looked down. "You killed her! You killed my sister!"

"No ... I ... it was an accident. Grace, please. I didn't mean to ..."

"You killed my sister! I'm telling!"

Addison was so caught up in the vision, she almost didn't hear her name being called. "Addison .... Addison! Someone's coming."

No, not now. Not when she was so close. She needed to see the rest, see how it all ended.

"You have to hide!" Vivian warned. "Hurry!"

Addison lifted her hands from the window frame. The attic door opened and Rose walked in, a Winchester bolt action rifle aimed at Addison's chest. "Don't move."

"Rose, I—"

"I knew it! I just knew there was something off about you!"

"Please. I meant no harm."

"How did you get in here ... into *my* house, into *my* attic?"

"Through an open window."

"I don't have *open* windows. All of my windows are sealed and locked. Unless ..." Rose's voice trailed off, pondering the possibilities. "I should have known. You opened one of them earlier today, didn't you? What were you trying to do, rob me? Well, joke's on you. I don't keep anything of value in here anymore."

"I wasn't trying to rob you."

"How did you manage to get in here?"

Addison slid a hand partway inside her jacket then stopped when she heard the action of the bolt putting a shell in the chamber.

"Utt … utt … uhh …" Rose mocked her. "You keep those hands where I can see 'em."

"I was just going to give you the key."

"What do you mean 'give me the key'? The key was lost ages ago."

"I found it."

"When?"

"Today."

"Where?"

"Behind some books in the library. If you'd just let me reach into my jacket, I'll get the key and show you."

Rose shook her head. "You'll do nothing of the kind. Not another word. I'm calling the police."

"If you could just hear me out, I'll tell you—"

Rose stepped forward, pressing the butt of the rifle against Addison's chest. "Not. Another. Word."

CHAPTER 19

A call to the local police was made. Rifle still poised and ready, Rose placed the call on speaker, explained the "emergency" and offered her home address. The male voice on the other line rattled off some additional questions and then asked Rose to remain on the line. To Addison's amazement, she didn't. She snapped her flip-phone closed and pushed it back inside her pocket.

"I hate these things, you know?" Rose said. "These cell phones."

Addison's reaction was to remain quiet, smile and nod, and prepare herself for what came next. With the police in transit, there was no need to make things worse than they already were. She'd made a mess of it all, and no quick fix or well-crafted remark would save her this time.

Vivian remained in the room beside Addison, her eyes squinted, like she was thinking, formulating a plan. "Tell her I'm glad she redid my room. She sews in there now."

Addison considered the request then shook her head, knowing what a dangerous thing it would be to mess with a woman who not only held a loaded gun in her hand, but who wouldn't believe her anyway. There was no point in saying anything.

"What are you doing?" Rose asked. "Why are you bobbing your head around?"

"Sorry. No reason."

"There must be a reason." Rose's eyes darted around the room. "You're not alone, are you? Who's with you? Your boyfriend Luke?"

"It's just me. I came alone. He doesn't even know I came here."

Rose ignored her, hollered, "Whatever you're planning, Luke. Don't bother. Take one step into this room, and I'll shoot."

"I told you, he's not here. I can call him if you'd like, prove to you he's not with me."

"The only thing calling him would prove is that he isn't in this room. Just how stupid do you think I am?"

"I don't. I just thought it would put you at ease."

"At ease? You must be joking. You broke into my house tonight. And if someone as scrawny as you can do it, imagine who else can. I don't think I'll ever be at *ease* again."

"Can I ... ask you something?"

"Do I have a choice?"

Addison took a deep breath in. "You like to sew, right?"

"*That's* what you wanted to ask me? You were shown around earlier. You're well aware I have a sewing room."

"It used to be Vivian's room."

That did it. Rose's eyes almost doubled in size. "Don't play with me, child. Whatever you're trying to do here, it won't work. And it's not funny."

Vivian pressed a finger to her lips. "Tell her the new wallpaper's nice, but I like the old paper better. The one with bright pink and orange flowers on it."

Addison inhaled a lungful of air. This was crazy, too much, far too much. She couldn't. Or ... could she?

Beneath Rose's jaded, acrimonious layers was a woman who'd hardened after losing her precious daughters, a woman who may have been giving and kind until her life took an unexpected turn.

Maybe what the moment needed was a dose of the erratic.

"I can sometimes communicate with those who are no longer living."

Rose's jaw fell open. "Don't. Don't say what I think you're about to say."

"The new wallpaper is nice," Addison said. "But Vivian liked the old paper better."

"Stop this," Rose warned.

"Pink and orange flowers. They were—"

"Enough!"

Sirens sounded below.

"Cops are here," Rose said. "Why not tell them your cockamamie story? Get yourself thrown in a place with a bunch of other kooks. Works for me."

Addison turned to Vivian. "I don't know what else to do, Vivian. I tried. And I'm sorry. I'll keep trying."

Rose gripped Addison by the arm, tossing her toward the attic door. "I've had enough. Shut your trap and get downstairs."

CHAPTER 20

"Mrs. Clark, I'm Officer North, and this is Officer Shumaker," Officer North said. "Are you all right?"

"I'm fine."

"We've done a full sweep of your place. We didn't find anyone else. So either she was alone as she stated or whoever was with her is gone. You can put the rifle down now, ma'am. You're safe."

Rose placed the rifle on the coffee table next to her. "I won't feel safe until you've hauled her away. There's something wrong with this one. She's not right … in the head. Talk to her for a few minutes. You'll see what I mean. She's loony. Tried to get me to believe she speaks to the dead, if you can believe it."

Officer North flashed Addison a look implying he thought he might have a little more than an average break-in on his hands. "You mind explaining why you broke in to this woman's house tonight?"

"I ... umm ... I was here earlier today, taking a tour of the house, and I ..."

And I, nothing.

There wasn't anything to say.

Not this time.

A sting of regret poured through her. Regret for not telling Luke. Not trusting he'd understand. Handcuffs were applied, and her Miranda rights were read to her. She was then escorted out the front door. Arms folded, and eyes stern, Rose followed close behind.

Vivian stood just outside the front door, a single tear trailing down her rosy cheek. Addison passed within a few inches of her, turned, and tried to offer a slight smile as a means of comfort. When she did, she noticed something. It wasn't Vivian standing there. It was Grace. Seeing Grace up close, she could finally tell them apart. Vivian had a small birthmark on the side of her neck. Grace didn't.

Fists clenched into balls at her side, Grace yelled, "You have to do something! You can't leave! Everyone leaves!"

Grace's turning point had come too late.

"I'm sorry," Addison whispered. "I'm so sorry."

The tears streamed now—wild and angry. Furious.

And then Grace screamed.

And screamed.

And screamed.

Something unusual happened. Officer North paused for a moment, his eyes darting around almost like he'd heard a sound he couldn't quite explain.

Grace leaned her back against the house's exterior and sagged to the floor. Vivian reappeared and sat next to her sister, whispering something in her ear.

Voice unsteady, Grace said, "Tell Mama I'm sorry I spilled soda all over my blue dress before the party. I didn't mean to. It was an accident."

No. Not again. Not this time. The new paint. The wallpaper. It hadn't worked before. There was no reason to believe it would be any different this time.

"Tell her!" Grace demanded.

Addison shook her head.

"Look," Rose pointed. "There she goes. She's doing it again!"

"What is it?" Officer North asked. "What are you doing?"

"Nothing," Addison replied. "I thought I felt a bug crawling on me. I must have been mistaken."

Officer Shumaker opened the door to the patrol car. Addison arced her head back, taking one last look at Vivian and Grace. The anguish of it all hit her, gushing like a seismic wave. She'd let them down.

"Rose," Addison yelled.

Rose bent down and smiled, pleased to see Addison in the back of the police car at last. "What is it now?"

"Grace is sorry she spilled soda all over her blue dress."

"What ... did ... you ... say?"

"She didn't mean to. It was an accident."

CHAPTER 21

The sound of metal bars clanking together in front of her felt like the last nail being driven into a steel, six-by-eight coffin. Addison had never felt so trapped, so helpless, so desperate to taste the kind of freedom she'd always taken for granted.

Of course, she had no one to blame but herself.

The details from the night Vivian and Grace died were clearer now, but there were still so many holes to plug. How to plug them was just as much of a mystery as figuring out how Grace fell from the attic window after what now appeared to be Vivian's accidental death. To get to the truth, she'd need to know the identity of everyone in the room at the time of the twins' deaths. And to find one person willing to provide her with answers.

Down the other end of the rectangular hallway, a familiar female voice found its way into Addison's cell. Lia McReedy, a medical examiner she'd met months before at Grayson Manor. What was she doing here?

Addison wrapped her hands around the bars of the cell and shouted, "Lia?"

Addison heard Lia say, "Who's in holding?"

A male voice answered, "Ahh, I don't know. We busted some chick for breaking and entering. Let's see … says here her name is Addison Lockhart. Know her?"

Several seconds later, a perplexed Lia stood in front of Addison's cell. A few inches shorter than Addison, Lia had chocolate brown hair cut into a bob, and wore colored contacts to accentuate her already stunning blue eyes. Every time Addison saw her, she was always dressed the same way—in black leggings and oversized boat neck T-shirts that showed off her ample bosom while flattering her midsection enough to disguise a small bump Addison assumed wasn't a pregnancy.

"How's your grandmother?" Lia asked. "Are you still telling people you don't know where she is?"

"I haven't heard from her in a while. It's true."

"Even though she covered up what happened at Grayson Manor decades ago, I doubt anyone cares about it anymore. She doesn't need to stay away. The case was closed months ago."

Addison felt the same. Unfortunately, her grandmother didn't agree.

"I'm surprised to see you here."

"Why?" Lia asked.

"I thought you were the ME in Rhinebeck."

"I'm the ME for Dutchess County. It includes Pleasant Valley *and* Rhinebeck."

"What happened in Pleasant Valley to bring you here?"

Lia avoided the question. "You're the last person I'd expect to see behind a cell. I heard you broke into someone's place?"

Addison nodded. "Yeah, it's a long story."

Lia glanced at her watch. "I've got time. Maybe I can help you. I have a hard time believing you're a criminal. Besides, you helped me out of a bad situation once."

She was right. Addison had almost forgotten rescuing Lia from a jaded ex-boyfriend months earlier.

"It sounds a lot worse than it is. I had a good reason for doing what I did."

"Which is?"

"Earlier today, my boyfriend Luke and I were given a tour of Rosecliff Manor."

Lia's eyes shifted from Addison to the floor, and she began gnawing on the inside of her bottom lip. "Why were you on a tour of Rosecliff? I know the owner. Shrewd woman. She's not the type to open her house to strangers."

"You're right. She had no interest in showing us the house. Then her son Derek showed up, and everything changed."

"How does this end with you being locked up?"

"I returned to the house tonight and let myself in without Rose's permission."

"Why?"

"During the tour, I wanted to see the attic," Addison said. "I was told it was locked, that the key had been lost a long time ago. I found it."

"What do you mean you found it?"

"When I was taking the tour, I found it in the library."

"And you didn't hand it over?"

Addison shook her head.

"Why not?" Lia asked.

"I knew if I did, Rose still wouldn't let me see the attic."

"What's this obsession you have with the attic? I mean, everyone around here knows the story, but what does it have to do with you?"

"I was looking for evidence."

"What kind of evidence?"

Prepped and curious, Lia was right where Addison wanted her to be. The bomb was ready to drop. "I don't believe the deaths of Vivian and Grace were accidents. Not entirely. And you want to know what else I think? You don't believe they were accidents either."

CHAPTER 22

In no time, Lia shifted from curious to defensive. "I have no idea what you're talking about or why you'd even say something like that. All I can say is, your assumption is wrong. I don't even know much about that case."

"You do know Thomas Gregory though, don't you?" Addison asked.

She paused before responding. "He's the guy who wrote the book about the town's history."

"He's also the guy who said he suspected the cops could have done a better job, among other things."

"So?"

"So ... do you know him, or don't you?"

"I ... like I just said, I know he wrote the book."

"Oh, I think you know him a lot better than that, Lia."

Lia took a step back. "Why are you saying this?"

"I saw your picture at his house. It was in a little frame he'd leaned against the windowsill. I almost didn't recognize you at first, but that's because the first time I met you at Grayson Manor, your hair was blond. Now it's brown, just like in the picture I saw."

Lia looked at Addison like she was trying to decide if she wanted to continue the charade. "Okay, maybe I know Tom a bit more than I let on."

"I don't just think you know him ... I think you gave him the idea to write about the girls in the first place. I mean, he's passionate about his convictions, but something else is driving him, or *someone* else. You."

Lia stepped forward again until the only thing separating her face and Addison's was the metal bars between them. "Keep your friggin' voice down!"

"Why? Who cares if anyone hears?"

"I care."

"I'm not trying to get you in trouble, Lia. I wouldn't. We're on the same page here. I want answers as much as you do. And what would really help me right now is if you told me what you know that everyone else doesn't."

"I don't get it. Why are you involved? Why does it matter to you?"

"I could ask you the same thing."

The rubber soles of a guards shoes squeaked their way toward Addison's cell. The guard fumbled around his pocket for a key, inserted it into the hole, jerked his head to the side, and grunted, "You're out of here, Lockhart."

"I can leave? Already?" Addison asked. "How?"

"Dunno. I was just sent back here to get you."

"Looks like you made bail," Lia said. "I have to go."

The guard turned, heading the same direction he came from. Halfway back, he turned, "You comin' or what?"

Before Addison could go after her, Lia had already disappeared into another room. Addison followed the guard back to the office, nervous to face Luke when she rounded the corner. Would he be angry? Would he understand? Her nervousness led to uncontrollable chatter, and she found herself saying to the guard, "I guess my boyfriend came to get me."

The guard turned, "I don't know nothin' about your boyfriend. All I know is, he's not the reason you're free."

CHAPTER 23

"Rose, what are you doing here?" Addison asked.

Rose sat in a chair in front of Officer North's desk. Neither looked pleased.

"I've dropped the charges," Rose said. "You're free to go."

"I ... don't understand?"

Rose snapped the clasp on the front of her purse shut and stood. "What's to understand? I've explained everything to the police, and they've agreed to let you go. You shouldn't be babbling on. You should be happy."

What had Rose explained?

And how?

And *why*?

Any story Rose had given in an effort to undo the damage would have been fabricated, a consequence that could have Rose facing her own criminal charges. It was a risky move either way.

"What did you say to get me released?"

Rose gave Addison a look that said she couldn't fathom why Addison couldn't leave well enough alone and keep her mouth shut. "As I explained to Officer North, in talking to my son tonight, I learned you left your wallet at the house earlier today when you stopped by. He'd tried calling to let me know you were on your way, but I was already in bed and didn't answer. He told you where the spare key was and advised you to pop in and out without waking me, which, of course, you did, until your overly nosey nature led you to the attic. No matter now. I know you meant no harm."

It was, of course, a well-orchestrated lie.

Addison thanked Rose and turned her attention to the waiting room and to Luke, whose pained expression made it clear just how hurt he was over the ordeal. "Luke, I—"

"Let's not talk about this now," he said. "Let's get you home."

She nodded, and nodded, and nodded, the only thing she could do to keep from falling apart.

Addison and Luke descended the steps in front of the police station. Rose followed close behind. "I'd like to speak to Addison. Alone."

Luke looked at Rose. "It's the middle of the night."

"It is, and we're all tired. I could have left her in jail tonight, and I didn't. I'm sure Addison's aware I didn't come here as some kind of Good Samaritan."

"I'm aware," Addison replied.

"We've all been through a lot tonight," Luke said. "If I promise she'll stop by in the morning, can it wait?"

"It cannot," Rose said. "Why don't you run along, Luke? I'll see she gets home all right."

CHAPTER 24

Luke did not agree to "run along," as Rose suggested, but he did offer an alternative solution. Rose could drive Addison home in her vehicle while Luke followed behind. He wasn't letting Addison out of his sight. Good deed or not, it wasn't up for negotiation.

Rose's car was an older model Cadillac in pristine condition. Addison opened the passenger-side door, slid across the tan leather seats, and buckled up. "Your son didn't have anything to do with this, did he?"

"He's not aware of any of it. And I have no interest in telling him either. He'd just fuss and coddle me until I suffocate. I figure if I'm wrong about you, if you are a criminal, well, I can always blow your head off if you try for round two."

At least she was honest. "Thank you for helping me."

"I'm not helping you. I'm helping myself. I thought the two of us could have a chat while I drove you home."

Rose was different now, not only in tone of voice, but in expression, like she'd shed one of her thick outer layers and lowered her guard.

"What would you like to ask me?"

Rose put the car in drive and pulled onto the road, the reflection of Luke's familiar headlights glistening in Addison's passenger-side mirror while they drove along.

"I'm a skeptic, you know," Rose said. "Someone who doesn't believe in life after death. I was raised a nonbeliever. It's the only truth I've ever known. And yet, part of me wants to believe you. Who knows why? I struggled to get back to sleep tonight, and I imagined I'd spend the rest of my nights much the same way if I didn't at least hear what you have to say."

"Are you saying you believe what I told you before, about the curtains and the stain on Grace's dress?"

"I'm saying, I'm not closed to it. Not entirely. Still, you'll have to convince me."

"How?"

"If you can communicate with Viv and Grace, prove it. I'll tell you something only they will know."

"I want you to believe me, but it doesn't work like that."

"Why not? Aren't you some kind of medium? Aren't you supposed to be able to conjure things up whenever you like?"

Addison shifted in her seat, facing Rose. "I see the girls when they want to be seen. It's not up to me. It's up to them."

Rose sighed. "You realize this isn't helping you any, right?"

"Think of it this way—if I was a fake, wouldn't I at least try to give you what you're asking?"

Rose turned onto the freeway. "Tell me how it works then. What happens when you do see them? Tell me straight. Assuming I might believe you, how is it you came to be in the lives of my girls, and just what do you mean to accomplish by breaking into my house?"

"The first time I saw your girls was at a funeral several months ago. I was there for someone else. I looked over, and they were chasing each other around your husband's grave. At the time, I didn't realize they weren't alive."

"When did you?"

"They appeared to me again several days ago, this time in a dream they seemed to be controlling. I saw the past, your manor, your husband's car, the cat."

"How old are they now? What do they look like?"

Addison answered her questions, giving the most detailed description she could about the girls' hair, their dresses, anything to justify what she had seen was real.

"What are they like?" Rose asked. "What do they say to you when they talk to you?"

"I've only seen them a few times. Vivian usually does all the talking. Grace hides."

To Addison's surprise, Rose let out a slight giggle. "She was always the skittish one of the two. Afraid of everything, she was."

"I don't think she understands what happened to her like Vivian does."

"You mentioned the stained dress earlier, and I'll admit, it got me thinking. No one else knew I changed their clothes that day. Their father was still at work, and their brother was at a neighbor's house. What I don't understand is, how did you manage to get the key to the attic? It's been missing for ages."

Though reluctant, Addison squeaked out, "Shadow showed me."

"The damn cat?"

Addison nodded.

"You're saying, not only am I supposed to believe you see my dead children, you see dead cats too? What about my husband? Any visits from him?"

"This isn't a joke, Mrs. Clark. I know it sounds like one, but it isn't. Not to me, and not to your daughters."

"Why have they come to you? What do they want?"

They wanted what any deceased person wanted—the ability to move on.

"Do you believe in heaven?" Addison asked. "In any kind of afterlife?"

"For my children's sake, and my husband's, and any chance I have of seeing them again, I have no choice. No matter what my own parents taught me, I have to."

"Your girls are still here, trapped somehow, unable to move on."

"Why?"

"I don't know. I suspect it has something to do with the night they died. Something unresolved."

"Why come to you? What can you do about it?"

Addison took a deep breath and said, "I can find out how they really died."

CHAPTER 25

Rose hadn't even flinched when Addison alluded to Vivian's and Grace's deaths being more than a mere accident. She kept her hands gripped to the wheel, looking straight ahead, without talking. The silence was unsettling and also telling. What did Rose know that Addison didn't?

It wasn't until Rose had parked in front of Grayson Manor that she mentioned her daughters again. "I feel them sometimes, you know? At least, I tell myself I do. At times it's like if I make the slightest turn, I'll run right into one of them."

"Just because you can't see something, doesn't mean it's not there."

"At first I thought I'd created their presence in my mind, convinced myself they were still with me because I was desperate for it to be true. Those early days, I was consumed with their deaths, unable to experience any kind of a life without them. Years passed, and although they never went out of my mind completely, I finally found a way to heal, to stop thinking of them every moment of every day."

Addison looked Rose in the eye. "Do you believe me now?"

"Let's just say, I'm more open than I was before."

"What do *you* think happened to your daughters? Do you believe their deaths were an accident?"

Rose fiddled with the zipper pull on the top half of her jacket, zipping it up and down. "I don't know, Addison. When they died, I was desperate for someone to blame. It's how I lost all my friends, you know. They all thought I'd gone mad. The police closed the case, and everyone wanted to move on. And why shouldn't they? It wasn't their children they lost. It was mine."

"If I could get to the truth of what happened, the *real* truth, would you help me?"

"Help you how?"

"The police concluded Vivian and Grace fell after trying to retrieve the doll from the roof. I asked Vivian about the doll. She had no recollection of it, which means either she can't remember or she never played with the doll that night."

"The doll belonged to Grace. I'd given it to her the prior Christmas. She never showed much interest in the doll, so I stored it in the attic along with a box of other toys. When police found it, I thought they'd dug it out of the box that night and decided to play with it, like an old toy they'd found a renewed interest in. How it came to be on the roof is a mystery. My girls were intelligent, neither one ignorant. I never believed they climbed out the window over a silly doll."

"I can tell you this—they weren't alone in the attic the night they died."

Rose entwined her fingers together in her lap. "How could you possibly know? Did they tell you?"

Addison had already admitted to seeing ghosts. Why not throw a vision into the mix?

"Sometimes when I touch things, certain objects, I'm able to see into another time."

"What are you saying? You have the ability to travel through time?"

"In a way. I can't alter an event or prevent it from happening. What's done is done. I'm more of a fly on the wall."

"And you've had a vision about that night?"

"I have. The girls were playing hide-and-seek, and they weren't alone. There was at least one other person in the attic at the time."

"Who? What did he look like?"

Addison described him.

"Hmm. Could be any number of teenage boys," Rose said. "They all wore their hair in a similar fashion back then. Even my Derek. You didn't ever see his face?"

Addison shook her head.

"The game stopped when Vivian found something that belonged to the boy—something he was embarrassed of when he found out she had it."

"Do you know what it was?" Rose asked.

"Paper, maybe pages from a magazine. They were folded up like he had them in his pocket. They must have fallen out while they were playing. Vivian was teasing the boy. He asked for the papers back. She said no. She ran across the room, held the papers out the window, and pretended to drop them. The boy leaned in, snatched them away, and Vivian fell out the window."

Rose's head jerked from side to side like she was picturing it all in her mind. "The pages, could you see them? What they were like?"

"Ripped on one side, smooth on the other."

Rose clasped a hand over her mouth. "Ripped ... like they'd been torn from a magazine."

"What is it?"

"I've kept you too long, Addison. You hurry up to bed and get some sleep. I'm going to give you my number. Call me tomorrow, okay?"

CHAPTER 26

It was two o'clock in the afternoon when Luke poked his head inside the bedroom door and whispered, "Lia McReedy's at the door."

Addison half-opened one eye and looked at him. She'd seen his lips moving, but was unclear about what he'd just said. "What did you say?"

"Remember the medical examiner from several months back? She's downstairs."

"Yeah," Addison said, propping herself into a sitting position. "I saw her last night."

"You … ahh … didn't mention it to me."

She hadn't mentioned it because he'd prevented her from doing so, choosing to go straight to bed when they arrived home hours before. She'd scooted beside him in bed, tapped him on the shoulder, asked if he was awake.

No response. She told herself he was already asleep, even though she knew better.

"There are a lot of things we need to talk about," Addison said. "I want you to know how sorry I am about everything. I never should have gone to Rosecliff Manor without telling you. If I could take it back, I would."

Luke rubbed a hand across his jaw. He seemed disappointed. Angry even. "I've never once given you a reason to doubt me, Addison. Last night when I realized you weren't next to me, realized you weren't even in this house, I called your cell phone. Did you answer? No. I got your voicemail. How would you feel if you were trying to get in touch with the person you love, and … you know what? I can't do this. I can't talk about this right now."

He turned.

"Luke, wait."

It was too late. He'd already walked out, closing the bedroom door behind him.

Addison flung the covers to the side and hopped off the bed, picking a pair of sweat pants off the floor and pulling them over her bare legs. She twisted her hair into a ponytail, passing the bedroom mirror without glancing into it. She didn't need to. She knew how hammered she looked.

When she descended the stairs, she saw Lia perched on the far end of the couch, hands interlaced over her lap.

"Did you see where Luke went?" Addison asked.

She pointed to the front door. "He walked out a few seconds ago. He seemed irritated. Is everything okay?"

Addison sat across from her. "I don't know. I hope so."

"Tom is my boyfriend," Lia blurted.

"Yeah, I kind of figured when I saw your picture."

"I don't even know why I'm telling you. When his book came out, he took all the heat for everything he said about the Clark twins. Never once mentioned me, or my involvement."

"He's trying to protect you."

"I guess so. I've never been in a decent relationship. I mean, I've dated a lot of guys, but they all turned out to be self-absorbed pricks. It's hard to find a good guy these days, you know? Tom is almost too good to be true."

She did know. Luke had loved her in a way no one ever had. In return, she'd pushed him away. "Tom seems like a great guy."

"He is. I'm the screw-up."

"Trust me. Right now, you couldn't possibly be the screw-up I am."

Lia smiled. "Thanks, but, I should have never put Tom in the position he's in."

Suggesting she'd put him in a position at all was an admission of something.

"What has people so enraged? Tom told me the older people in the community questioned his motives for saying what he did. It's been several decades. Why do people care if another theory is put forward now?"

"Some see it as an attack on the police department. He pointed a finger, said they didn't do their job. Pleasant Valley is a town, not a city. They band together. They don't appreciate outsiders coming in and making accusations."

Addison leaned back, crossed one leg over the other. "Are you going to tell me why you wanted Tom to say what he did in his book?"

Lia paused.

"Lia, you can trust me."

"I ... okay. My grandfather worked on the original investigation."

"He was one of the investigating officers?"

She shook her head. "He was an ME, just like I am. When he looked over the twins' bodies, he couldn't find any evidence of foul play, but their deaths ... they just seemed off somehow."

"Did he try talking to anyone about it?"

"He talked to everyone. He pushed to keep the case open when the police wanted it closed. He went to the family, talked to everyone there that night. The fact he wouldn't let it go pissed off a lot of people."

"When you say *people*, are you referring to the Clarks?"

"He took a lot of heat from the cops working the investigation at the time. They were convinced my grandfather was trying to say they were incompetent, just like Tom is doing now. My grandfather wasn't incompetent. He was just trying to pick up where they left off, see what he could find out on his own time."

"Did he discover anything suspicious?" Addison asked.

"Most people he talked to were tight-lipped, too nervous to talk about it. My grandfather suspected it was because what happened was so tragic, everyone wanted to put it far from their minds."

"I imagine your grandfather is retired. Why resurrect his suspicions now? Why is it so important to you?"

"A year after the case was closed, my grandfather continued to bring the twins up in conversation when he could. At that point, even the sheriff was sick of hearing it. My grandfather was fired. He went to work for another county, but Vivian and Grace were always in the back of his mind. Last year, he died. A few weeks before his death he admitted his one regret was never finding out what really happened to the Clark girls." She glanced out the window. "Now you know my story. What's yours? Why are you so interested in the Clark girls?"

Addison liked Lia. She had since the first time they met, when she'd followed her into the wooded area behind her house and was told to steer clear of the crime scene. She even imagined the two could be friends. But right now didn't seem like the time to bond over stories of visions and spirits. "I read Tom's book. It piqued my interest."

"Piqued it enough to break into Rose's house? Oh, come on. Tell me there's more to it. There has to be."

Addison despised lying, but having no other choice, she blurted the first thing that popped into her head. "I'm writing a book too."

"You're what?"

"When we first met, and Roxanne Rafferty's body was discovered, it made me wonder how many other unusual or unsolved cases there are in New York. I did some research. Turns out, there are quite a few."

"You didn't mention your book to Tom when you spoke to him."

"I didn't want to offend him, or for him to feel like I'm using him for information."

"That's exactly what you're doing, isn't it?"

"I'm only trying to find more stories like Roxy's and bring them to light."

The sound of the clock on the mantle ticking seemed to go on forever while Addison waited, hoping Lia would believe what she'd just told her. When she couldn't bear the silence any longer, she said, "I'd like to help you find the answers you're looking for—prove your grandfather was right."

"Why? So you can take all the credit in your story?"

"I won't take any of the credit. I'll give all the credit to him."

"What makes you think you can get anywhere? All Tom managed to do was to make people angry."

"He did more than you think. He got people talking, got them thinking about it again."

"People like who?"

"Rose Clark. She's always had her suspicions."

"How do you know?"

"I talked to her."

"Wait a minute. She's the one who had the charges dropped, isn't she?"

Addison smiled. "She is. We talked, and I'm hoping everything's fine now."

"You *talked*? I didn't think Rose talked to anyone."

"For over an hour."

"Well? What did she say?"

"I'll make you a deal. You tell me what you know, and I'll tell you what I know."

"And then?"

"Then I find our murderer."

CHAPTER 27

A rush of fetid air swirled around Addison, clogging her lungs, making it almost impossible to breathe. Something felt off. Cold. Expired. Clutching the kitchen counter's edge, she steadied herself and hung on, desperate for the moment to pass. It didn't. Time ticked by, each second making her feel more and more weighted down.

The front door opened and closed.

Addison attempted to circle around, but couldn't. She was stuck. Paralyzed. Unable to move. She opened her mouth, trying to form a single word: help.

Then two words: *help me.*

Had anyone heard her? Was anyone listening?

Luke stepped in front of her. "Addison, what's wrong? Talk to me. What's going on?"

"I … can't …"

He wound his fingers around her arms and pulled, forcing her to release her grip on the counter. She fell forward, collapsing into him.

Luke wrapped his arms around her, holding her tight. "Talk to me. What's happening?"

"It's Helen."

"Helen Bouvier?" Luke asked. "Our neighbor?"

Addison nodded.

"Something's wrong, Luke. She's not all right. I can feel it."

"Did you have a vision?"

"I … not today. When I went to her house to ask about Cliff Clark, I touched her cane, and I blacked out for a minute. I had flashes of a vision, something that hadn't happened yet, something still to come. I didn't know …"

"Didn't know what?"

"I had no way of knowing it would happen this soon or I would have done something to help her."

"Addison, what did you see?"

"Helen on her bed in her room. Her eyes were closed. Milton was standing over her. He was crying. She was dead."

CHAPTER 28

Addison turned the knob and walked inside the house. "Helen, are you here? It's Addison and Luke. We're coming in."

The house remained still, the only sound coming from the drip of a leaky faucet in the kitchen. Addison looked around. The living room was empty. The kitchen was empty.

"Where's her bedroom?" Luke asked.

Addison entered the hallway. "I think it's down here."

Entering Helen's room, the set-up mimicked her vision. Helen was on the bed. A blanket covered most of her body and folded down under her chin. Milton stood over Helen, his eyes filled with tears.

"Milton?" Luke asked. "What's happened?"

Milton didn't move, didn't look up. "She's dead."

"How?" Luke pressed.

Milton fisted his hands around the edges of a pillow he held to his chest and squeezed. "I ... had to, you see. I had no choice. I ... I loved her."

Luke and Addison exchanged horrified glances.

Addison took a step toward Milton, hoping to bypass him, check for a pulse. Luke reached forward, catching her hand in his. She glanced back.

Luke stepped in front of Addison, his body acting as a shield between her and Milton. "We don't know what happened here yet. Hang back a minute."

Addison nodded.

"Milton, I need you to move so I can see if she's still alive," Luke said.

"She isn't."

"Move, Milton."

"No ... I can't."

"You can either move, or I'll move you."

With his shoulders turned in, Milton backed away from Helen.

Luke reached over, pressing two fingers to the side of her neck.

"Do you feel anything?" Addison asked. "Does she have a pulse?"

Luke frowned. "No."

Addison looked at Milton who was now hunched in the corner, his body rocking back and forth. "Milton, did you do it? Did you kill her?"

Milton began rambling, "I had no choice ... I had no choice ... I had no choice."

"What do you mean?"

Had he snapped, become angry, and killed her? Looking at Milton now, at the pillow still clutched in his hands like a child's security blanket, the truth of what had transpired was clear. "Milton, did you suffocate her?"

He didn't respond.

Addison persisted. "Answer me, Milton! Did. You. Suffocate. Her?"

Luke pulled his phone out of his pocket. "I'm calling the police."

"Put the phone down, Luke," a female voice echoed from the bathroom.

Luke and Addison turned, both staring at the woman who'd just stepped out of the bathroom. The woman directed her attention at Addison. "You mustn't blame Milton. He's not to blame for Helen's death. I am."

CHAPTER 29

Dressed in a long skirt, a navy V-neck shirt and a jean jacket vest, Marjorie Grayson leaned against the bathroom door. Her usually impeccably applied make-up was smeared around her eyes. In one hand, she held a washcloth. It was stained black.

"Marjorie, what are you doing here?" Addison asked.

"Hello, Granddaughter."

"I'm calling the police, Marjorie," Luke said. "I don't know what's going on, but the cops can deal with it."

Marjorie shook a finger at him. "You'll do nothing of the kind."

"Look, whether you're Addison's grandmother or not, I can't protect you from this, and I won't."

"Nor should you. If you'd allow me to explain, I believe we can sort this whole mess out."

"I'm not interested in anything you have to—"

"Luke, please," Marjorie said. "She's already passed. Surely you can spare another moment or two."

Luke pressed the end-call button on the phone. "Two minutes. Then I'm calling."

"Understood." Marjorie walked to a nearby chair, sat down. "A few months ago, Helen learned she had stage four breast cancer. She always hated hospitals, and by the time Milton forced her to go and it was detected, it was much too late. The cancer had already spread to her liver, her spleen, her bones. She was in pain. So much pain."

Addison thought back to her visit a few days before, to the cup of tea in Helen's unstable hand. "Weren't there treatments, something that could have helped her?"

"Although the prognosis was bleak, and she wouldn't have had much time left either way, the doctor suggested radiation. She refused."

"Why?" Addison asked.

"She'd witnessed the side effects firsthand. One of her friends died last year after a slew of procedures. None of them successful. Illnesses like this aren't so easy to treat when you get to be our age."

Marjorie stood, walked over to Helen's bedside table, and removed a series of documents. She handed them to Addison. "See for yourself. It's all in there. Her diagnoses, her life expectancy, the doctor's recommendations—all of it."

Luke leaned in, and together they scanned the pages.

What Marjorie said was true.

"But you *killed* her," Addison said. "No matter how sick she was ... how could you?"

Marjorie looked at Milton. "Give Addison the letter."

He reached into his back pocket, handing over a crumpled envelope. She broke the seal, withdrew the letter inside, and read it aloud.

Addison,

I realize now how unkind I was to you the other day, and I'd like to apologize. If you're receiving this letter, Milton has delivered it to your doorstep and has left Rhinebeck for good. It doesn't matter where he went, he won't be returning, so don't try to find him.

I'd like to impose on you now and ask you to call the police. Tell them you stopped by my house for a visit and found me in bed, deceased. Yes, I did say deceased. Burial instructions and all other pertinent information are in my will, so you needn't trouble yourself with any additional details.

Right now, I'm sure you're caught up in all of the "why" and "how" of my passing. Ever since you came to Rhinebeck, you seemed to have a knack for sticking your nose in everything. Truth is, I've always admired the quality in you. I also found it irritating. Maybe because it reminded me of your grandmother, and I must confess she's always been a true friend to me, despite what I said before.

You see, when I learned I was dying, I was angry, at everything and everyone. Then I came up with a way out, a way to be set free, relieved of the excruciating pain I experienced during the final days of my life. I know you don't understand. I don't expect you to. You've always been the girl with her heart set on doing the right thing.

Milton is not a killer. He's a savior. My savior. He couldn't stand to see me in pain any more than I could bear enduring it. I didn't just ask him to end my life, I begged him for it. I hope you understand.

And now if you'd be so kind to burn this letter, you will have my eternal gratitude.

Helen Bouvier

Addison refolded the letter and breathed, trying to take it all in.

"How do we even know she wrote that letter?" Luke asked.

"She wrote it," Addison replied. "I recognize the handwriting. When I first moved to Grayson Manor, she brought me a pie. It had a handwritten note attached to it. The writing on that note and on this letter is the same."

Luke wiped his brow. "It still doesn't make sense. The letter says Milton is the one responsible for Helen's death. Not Marjorie."

"You're right," Marjorie said. "Helen's original plan was to ingest a bottle of pills, fall asleep, and die peacefully."

"Why didn't she?"

"She tried. They made her ill. She vomited most of the night, but she lived. The next day, she beseeched

Milton, asked him to help her end her life. She didn't care how. He couldn't go through with it, so he called me. I flew in very early this morning, and here we are."

"No matter how much pain she was in, it doesn't give you the right to play God," Luke said. "It's not for you to decide. You could have taken her to the hospital or done something else, *anything* else ... not *this*."

"Put yourself in my place, Luke," Marjorie said. "Think about what you would do if it was Addison. If you knew she was going to die anyway, how long would you make her writhe in agony before even you gave in? Can you honestly say you wouldn't do whatever was necessary to bring her peace?"

Luke lowered his head, shaking it from side to side. "So what now? You were just going to what, walk out, leave us to deal with it?"

"On the contrary. I'm not going anywhere."

"You're not?" Addison asked.

"It's time I make my peace with my past. If it comes back to haunt me, so be it. I'd never leave my granddaughter to handle this on her own."

"She's not on her own," Luke shot back. "She has me. She'll *always* have me."

She'd always have him. Hearing those words was a huge relief.

"What now?" Addison asked. "We can't pretend none of this is happening. I'm not leaving Helen like this. It wouldn't be right."

"Who said anything about leaving her?" Marjorie said. "The conversation we need to be having is about what we're going to tell the police when they get here, and whether we're all planning to tell the same story." She shifted her gaze to Luke. "I know you're not pleased with what's happened here. Whatever you decide to do, I won't stop you. But we need to get our stories straight, for all our sakes."

Luke took what may have been the deepest and longest breath of his life. "When she's examined, won't the medical examiner be able to prove foul play was involved?"

"The ME may be able to prove asphyxia," Marjorie said. "But as to the proof she'll need, she won't get anywhere if we dispose of the pillow. So, Luke … what's it going to be?"

CHAPTER 30

After a lengthy amount of time spent soothing Milton's anguished heart, Marjorie finally pried the pillow from his hands. She disappeared for a short time then reemerged without it. A story was formed, and everyone agreed. The only thing left to deal with now was a tall, blubbering wild card, who looked like he was about to blow.

"Before the call is made, I want to be clear," Marjorie said. "If this doesn't go as planned, and the police decide one of us is to blame, I'll be turning myself in. I won't have it any other way, and none of you are to try to stop me. Understood?"

Addison and Luke nodded.

"Milton?" Marjorie asked. "Do you hear me? I need to know you understand."

Milton's head rose partway. "Yes, ma'am."

"All right then, it's settled. Who wants to make the call?"

Luke dialed the phone, remaining on the line while police were dispatched to their location. Marjorie and Addison moved to the living room, where they watched and waited.

"I don't believe it was you," Addison said.

"What do you mean?"

"Milton is torn up, more than he should be. It's not because Helen's gone, is it? You didn't do it. You didn't kill her. He did."

"Nonsense. You're allowing your mind to run rampant. Stick with the plan, Addison. Don't give it another thought."

"I felt her, you know, felt Helen pass through me the moment she died. You said you sent Milton to the store earlier so an alibi could be established for him if it came down to it. I felt Helen's death *after* Milton returned home."

"How would you know when he arrived back at the house?"

Addison thought back, remembered seeing Helen's car drive past her house. "I saw Milton in Helen's car earlier today."

"It doesn't mean he's to blame for what happened."

"But he is, isn't he? You don't have to take the fall for him. You don't have to protect him."

Marjorie clenched Addison's hand, patting it several times before speaking. "I see what you're trying to do here, Addison. We need to stick to the plan."

"Even if the plan backfires? You're really willing to turn yourself in?"

"To protect all of you, you bet I am. I'd never planned to involve you in the first place. I wasn't even going to give you the letter Helen wrote."

"You never *planned* to involve me? Did it ever occur to you to ask for my help, my opinion about all this before you put your plan into action?"

"Addison, please. Take a breath, take five if you need to. I don't want you all riled up when the cops get here. It won't help the situation. Milton was the one person in life Helen adored more than anyone. The one who remained by her side through it all. He doesn't deserve to spend the rest of his life behind bars for honoring her dying wish, does he?"

CHAPTER 31

Lia McReedy was beginning to think there was a lot more to Addison Lockhart than the doe-eyed, sweet-faced girl she made herself out of be. Wherever Addison went, death seemed to follow like a bad habit. Over the past five minutes she'd eavesdropped on Addison's conversation with Officer Waters and Jackson. Listened to the same regurgitated story Luke and Marjorie told. It was all a bit too coincidental for her liking. The only one who *wasn't* talking was the tight-lipped old man sitting at the kitchen table, staring at the floor. Too inconsolable to speak, no one had managed to get a word out of him.

Helen's body was lined out perfectly straight on the bed when Lia had walked in. A little too perfect. And her head was covered with a sheet. Maybe out of respect, maybe out of guilt. It was too early to tell. Lia aimed a pen at Albert, the crime scene photographer. "You get everything you need to in here? I'm ready to take a look at the body."

He snapped another picture. "Just a few more."

Officer Jackson entered the room, a man she also referred to as "Officer Pain in the Ass" on occasion, partially because he was her ex-boyfriend and partially because the shoe fit. He cleared his throat. She ignored him, using the edge of her pen to lift the edge of the sheet away from Helen's head.

Officer Jackson cozied up behind her, leaning so far forward the steam from his breath made the hair on her neck bristle.

She arched her body to the side.

He laughed.

"Still jumpy after all this time," he grunted.

"You don't have to get so close."

"You used to like it."

"TJ, I'm working here. Back off me."

He raised his hands in surrender. "Fine, fine. Just trying to be nice is all. Sheesh. What you thinkin'? She been dead long?"

"Not long. Couple hours maybe. Her muscles are starting to stiffen. The area around her eyelids has changed, but her neck still looks normal."

"Fits with the timeline Marjorie Grayson gave us."

"I bet it does," she said.

"What does that mean?"

"Nothing."

"It's never nothing with you."

"Right now it is."

"Am I the only one who finds it strange that the Lockhart girl has been in the center of more than one death over the last year?"

"She was Helen Bouvier's neighbor, TJ. It wasn't her fault a dead woman was found in her house when she inherited it."

"Yeah, well," he thumbed toward the door, "the mute out there at the table could have dialed 9-1-1 when he found her. He didn't. Instead I'm to believe he drove to the neighbor's house where Marjorie Grayson just happened to be visiting, the same woman involved in her own husband's death several decades ago."

"Allegedly," Lia said. "She was never charged."

"Still. You know what I mean."

"If you're looking for answers, maybe you should get out there and push the old dude to talk."

"Tryin' to get rid of me, McReedy?"

McReedy. She'd always been Lia until the day she ended their relationship. Now he only referred to her by her last name, his manipulative way of making her feel like she was nothing to him anymore. Good. It was about time he moved on.

"Not trying to get rid of you," she lied. "Just *trying* to do my job."

Instead of exiting the room, he leaned out the bedroom door, pointed, and said, "You. Come here."

Milton skulked into the bedroom, his legs unsteady, eyes glossed over in a haze.

"I'm gonna need you to tell me what went on here today," Officer Jackson said.

"Marjorie told you," Milton muttered.

"I don't want Marjorie Grayson's version. I want yours."

Marjorie entered the room. "What are you doing? Why have you brought Milton back here? Can't you see he's under distress?"

Officer Jackson curved his lips into a smile. "All due respect, I'm not talking to you right now. You had your turn."

Marjorie shoved Officer Jackson aside, looping an arm around Milton. "Fine. If Milton stays, I stay."

Lia glanced up, recognizing the look in Officer Jackson's eyes—the same look he always had when he was about to burst.

Officer Jackson reeled around. "Look at her, Milton. Look at Helen."

When Milton didn't do as requested, Officer Jackson prodded further. "Oh, come on now. You can do it. She was your friend, wasn't she? Aren't you the one who found her?"

Tears streaming down his cheeks, Milton looked at Marjorie.

Officer Jackson gripped Milton's jaw in his hand, twisting it to face Helen. "Don't look at Mrs. Grayson. Look at Helen. *Look at her!* Yesterday this woman was alive, full of life, full of color. Now she's a corpse, withering and rotting away, and you expect me to believe she just passed away in her sleep?"

In an attempt to keep Marjorie from being arrested for assaulting an officer, Lia said, "Take your hands off him, TJ. He hasn't done anything."

His hands remained. Lia called for backup, yelling for Officer Waters. Officer Waters entered the room and issued TJ a warning. This time he listened.

"If everyone could just calm down," Marjorie said. "I'd like to at least try to clear the air. You've all asked about her death, how she died, how we're involved. But no one has bothered to ask about Helen. She had cancer. And as you can see, she's not exactly a spring chicken. So before you make allegations, get your facts straight first."

CHAPTER 32

Two hours later, Marjorie, Addison, Luke, and Milton reconvened at Grayson Manor after Helen's body was taken by ambulance to be examined. To Addison, the waiting and the uncertainty of what Lia would find during the autopsy was the hardest.

Addison's cell phone vibrated inside her pocket. She pulled it out and answered.

"I was surprised I didn't hear from you today," Rose said.

"I meant to call," Addison replied.

"Then why haven't you?"

"My neighbor passed away several hours ago, and the day just got away from me."

"I'm sorry to hear that. Are you free now?"

"I am."

"Good. I spent the day putting together a list of names of everyone I can recall being invited to the Easter party. Then I listed their children. I found only two possibilities, two couples with boys matching the age and description of the person you mentioned in your ... whatever you call it. Grab a pen and paper and I'll give them to you."

She opened a drawer, fiddled around. Nothing to write on but the flip side of the utility bill. It would have to do. "Ready."

"Rick Snider and Dean Robertson."

There was, of course, a third boy Rose *hadn't* mentioned yet. Derek. Addison questioned whether Rose could even bring herself to suspect her own son. She must have.

"Any idea how old they were at the time?"

"Fifteen, sixteen, seventeen. Can't be sure exactly. They were both friends of my son. He was fifteen at the time."

Interesting.

"Any idea where they're living now?"

"I made some calls to their families, found out both of them are still living in New York. Rick lives in

Providence, and Dean lives in Stillwater. I have addresses. A home address for Rick, and a work address for Dean."

Addison jotted the addresses down.

"When you're free, I'd like to speak to you again," Rose said. "It doesn't have to be today."

"I'll get with you tomorrow after I've tracked down Rick and Dean."

"Any idea what you plan to say?"

"Whatever it takes to get some answers."

CHAPTER 33

Addison heard a knock at outside her bedroom door.

"Come in," Addison said.

Marjorie entered, closing the door behind her. "Who were you talking to just now?"

Addison reached inside a laundry basket, pulled out a shirt, folded it, then repeated the movement. "Just someone I'm helping out."

Marjorie crossed her arms in front of her, sat down on a chair at Luke's desk. "Tell me about it."

"We haven't seen each other for months, and then you turn up today and take a sudden interest in my life. I guess I don't understand why it's so important to you."

"I'm just trying to make conversation, catch up, see how you've been doing."

While it may have been true, it wasn't the only reason she'd asked.

"You know already, don't you?" Addison asked.

"That you've taken an interest in the Clark girls? I do. Milton told me."

"I'm guessing you know about my visit with Helen the other day?"

Marjorie crossed one leg over the other, resting a hand on her knee. "Among other things. When did the girls come to you?"

"How do you know they—"

"It's as I told you months ago, when your powers heighten, mine diminish. I can feel it. And I'm glad. I've seen all I need to see, helped those I needed to help. I'm ready to let it all go. I've been waiting a long time now."

"It doesn't bother you?"

"Why would it? You were born for this, and you've finally embraced it. I'm so proud."

"My life is ... complicated. Last week it was normal. Perfect. Now it's a mess. I don't know how to keep everything balanced."

"You're not alone, Addison. You have Luke. He seems plenty balanced to me."

"He is. He's perfect. I'm the one who's a mess."

"You know he loves you, right? I've never seen a man look at a woman the way he looks at you."

"Sometimes I think he deserves better, someone less complicated."

Marjorie shook her head. "Don't talk that way. What you are, who you are, the gifts you think make your life more difficult—those same gifts make you unique. Luke could spend the rest of his life searching for another girl like you. He'd never find her."

"Why have you decided to stay?"

"When Milton called me, told me about Helen, I started thinking about my own life. You're the only thing I have left, and I haven't even taken the time to get to know you. Who knows how long I have left—days, months, years? It's all ticking away. You're my legacy, our family's legacy. I want to be part of your life."

"Do you plan on staying for a while then?"

Marjorie nodded.

"And you're not worried about the cops picking apart your past now that you've returned?"

"Not anymore. Recently, I had a dream. I saw my own death, if you can believe it. It doesn't end with me behind bars. Now ... we've gotten way off topic. You've had another vision. Let's hear it."

Addison scooted the laundry aside and sat on the edge of the bed. "You're right, I have."

She filled her in on the recent events leading up to the current day.

When she finished, Marjorie said, "I fear you're putting yourself in danger with this one."

"Didn't you?"

"I did. Feels different now though—now that it's you."

"I'm determined to see it through. I have to for Vivian and Grace."

"In all my years, in all the visions I had, those shrouded in secrecy always got me in the most trouble."

"Are you telling me I should stop, that I shouldn't seek justice for those two girls?"

"I'm not *telling* you anything. I'm *asking* you to be cautious. And no matter what you do, you're better off with Luke at your side."

CHAPTER 34

Marjorie peeked through sheer curtains draped across Addison's bedroom window. "What's that Lia woman doing back here?"

Addison joined her grandmother. "Maybe she wants to talk to me about the Clark girls."

"Or *maybe* she's finished her autopsy."

"If she found anything incriminating, she wouldn't be alone, would she?"

It was a valid point, but not one Addison believed. Not entirely. She descended the stairs and opened the front door.

"Hey, Addison," Lia said. "Can we talk?"

Addison nodded and stepped outside. Marjorie followed.

"I ... ahh ... need to talk to Addison alone," Lia said.

Hands on hips, Marjorie replied, "What for?"

"Marjorie, please," Addison said. "Let me handle this."

"I think it's best if I stay," Marjorie said.

Lia clammed up, crossing her arms in front of her. She wasn't talking, not with Marjorie around. Marjorie sighed loud enough to indicate her frustration then pivoted and charged back inside the house.

Once they were alone, Lia said, "Is she always like this?"

"Seems like it. Truth is, I haven't known her for very long. I wasn't around her when I was a child."

"Why not?"

"She and my mother didn't get along. When my mother passed away last year. Marjorie reentered my life. Anyway, are you here about what we discussed earlier?"

"I'm here about Helen. Why do you ask? Has anything changed?"

"Rose called me. She gave me the names of a couple boys who were there the night of the party. It's possible they may have been playing in the attic with the girls. I realize no one admitted it before … but who knows? Maybe now someone will."

"Addison, I ... that's great. I came by because I wanted to tell you I spoke to Helen's doctor this evening."

"Oh?"

"Marjorie was right. She had cancer. He said she refused any kind of treatment. Were you aware of this?"

"She kept her illness from me," Addison said. "After she died, Marjorie told me."

"Are you familiar with cyanosis?"

"Cya ... what?"

"Cyanosis. It means 'the blue disease.'"

"Oh ... kay."

"It appears when the tissues near the skin's surface are low in oxygen. In Helen's case, in the discoloration I detected in the skin around her nose."

"Why are you telling me this?"

"Why wouldn't I? Aren't you interested?"

"Helen was my neighbor, and I'm sorry she's gone, but we weren't close."

"When I examined Helen, I noticed petechial hemorrhages in her skin. There was also some bruising inside Helen's mouth."

More terms Addison wasn't familiar with. "I assume you're telling me this because you're leading up to something."

"I don't believe Helen died in her sleep, or in some accidental way. I believe she was suffocated."

Addison did her best to keep a straight face. "Okay."

"Okay? I plan to put this information in my report."

Again, Addison said, "Okay."

"No, it's not okay. If you don't tell me what's going on right now, whatever your involvement is, I can't protect you."

Addison's legs wobbled, feeling like they were about to collapse beneath her. She clutched the porch railing to keep herself steady. "Even if I did know what was going on, and I'm not saying I do, why would you want to protect me? We don't even know each other. Not really."

"You seem like a good person. I believe you are a good person. I also believe you want to do what's right. But the more I'm around you, the more I notice how many situations you get yourself into. I may be naïve sometimes, but I'm not stupid. They can't *all* be a coincidence."

"I like you, Lia. And I appreciate you taking the time to stop by. I don't have a lot of friends here. I haven't made any since I moved, actually. You're a good person too. I knew it the first time we met. If I considered anyone a friend, it would be you."

Lia shielded her eyes with a hand. "So that's it? That's all you have to say?"

Addison nodded.

"This is your last chance. Whomever you're protecting, it isn't worth it. If the cops can prove Helen was suffocated, and it turns out you omitted information, *you* could be charged as an accessory, *Luke* could be charged as an accessory."

Without the pillow, which in this case was the proof they needed, what evidence did they have to form a case? None. Or was she wrong, fooling herself into believing everything would be all right? The more it festered, the more unsure she became.

Lia took her hand. "Your eyes are watering, Addison. Please, tell me."

"I ... I just really don't know if ..."

The front door opened and closed.

Busted.

Addison turned, expecting to find Marjorie and instead came face to face with Milton.

His voice calm, he said, "It was me. I did it. I killed her."

Eyes wide, Addison looked at Milton then Lia. "He's still in shock. He doesn't know what he's talking about."

"No, Addison, it's okay." He looked at Lia. "Addison, Luke, Marjorie ... they had no part in what happened to my Helen. If you want, I'll make a confession. Just, leave them out of it."

"Milton, don't," Addison said. "Stop."

"It's okay," Lia said. "I'm not the police."

"Then make a call," Milton said. "Get them down here. I'll tell them everything."

Lia took out her phone, dialed.

"Addison, I'm sorry," Milton said. "I have to. I can't live a lie. I just can't."

A frantic Marjorie bounded onto the porch, her steely gaze directed at Addison. "What have you done?"

CHAPTER 35

She hadn't *done* a thing, a moot point now. Officer Waters and Jackson returned to collect Milton, escorting him into the police vehicle while everyone else looked on. A bitter Marjorie shut herself away in one of Addison's guest rooms, refusing any company or the chance to let Addison explain what had actually happened.

Police gone, Lia made one final plea. "Now will you tell me what happened?"

Luke walked up behind Addison, smoothing his hands up and down her goose-fleshed arms. He leaned in, whispered, "Let's go inside. It's cold out here. We'll tell her together."

The three of them entered the house, gathering around the fire.

"What happened to Helen," Luke began, "wasn't our idea. We didn't even know she was ill until after she died."

Luke went on, telling Lia they'd stopped by Helen's house to question her about the Clark girls one more time. It was the only part of his story that wasn't entirely true, but admitting they'd stopped by after Addison had a hunch her neighbor was dead wasn't a viable option. He explained Helen was already dead when they arrived. How long, he didn't know. They'd been told Helen was already dying, in a lot of pain, enough pain to beg Milton to end her life. When he finished, Addison retrieved Helen's letter and handed it over to Lia.

"And this, what you've told me, it's the truth?" Lia asked. "All of it?"

"It is," Luke said.

Addison nodded in agreement.

Lia was silent for several seconds. "Did you know Milton took a bullet for Helen?"

"I didn't," Addison replied. "When?"

"Back when Helen Bouvier was known as Vivian Bouvier, the aspiring actress, she was in a western called *Ride the West Wind.* One of the extras, a man named

Don Torres, became interested in her. He followed her around before and after rehearsal. At first, she was polite, thinking it would wear off. It didn't. One night he caught her alone, and he kissed her. She rebuffed him and decided the best way to get rid of the unwanted attention was to flirt with one of the movie's producers. Don was angry, of course. He was convinced everyone knew about the rejection. The way he saw it, he was the butt of her joke. A few nights before the movie wrapped, she was one of the last people to leave the set. He stood behind a garbage container waiting for her to walk by. When she was close enough, he jumped out, pointed a revolver at her. She laughed, thinking the gun was a fake, one of the props used in the movie. When he pulled back on the hammer, she realized he was serious. Lucky for her, Milton was with her at the time. He shielded her body with his own, taking the bullet. It clipped him just under his rib cage."

"How do you know all this?" Addison asked.

"I'm obsessed with the show *Hollywood Near Misses.* Ever seen it?"

Addison shook her head.

"I've seen every episode. Helen's story was part of a special they ran one night during western-theme week. After we were in her house today and I saw all the signed actor photographs she had on her walls, I took a look at her paperwork, noticed the name Vivian as one of her former aliases, and made the connection."

"She never told me that story before," Addison said.

"The reason I'm bringing it up is, I want you to know it's not my intention to get anyone in trouble here. There's premeditated murder, and then there's this."

"What are you saying?"

"I believe Milton and Marjorie's story. Is it wrong in the eyes of the law? I suppose it is. I also know what it's like to see a person you care about endure the kind of pain Helen did."

"So, what happens next?"

"The pillow—where is it now?"

"We don't know. Neither one of us."

The declaration only left two people who might, Milton and Marjorie. Addison hoped Lia wouldn't press any further.

"If it turns up, it's likely saliva will be found, possibly blood and tissue cells too," Lia said. "I plan to speak to

Milton in the morning just to satisfy myself before I turn in my report. But here's a word of advice. Wherever the pillow ended up, make sure it's never found."

CHAPTER 36

Morning's pale radiance shone through the bedroom window. Addison rolled over and checked the time. Almost eight. An early riser, Luke was already gone.

Gone.

For a split-second, the thought of him leaving crossed her mind. And though she wanted to believe what they shared together was strong enough to withstand the events of the last week, she couldn't blame him if it had become too much.

Addison wound a robe around her body and walked downstairs. Looking around, it seemed she was alone.

"Luke, are you here?"

Silence.

She walked to Marjorie's room and knocked. "Marjorie, it's Addison. Can we talk?"

No answer.

Luke's truck pulled to a stop outside. He walked into the house clutching a paper sack in one hand. "Morning. Your grandmother's not in there."

"Where is she?"

He shrugged. "No idea. I knocked about an hour ago to see if she needed anything from the store. When she didn't answer, I cracked the door just a bit, called her name again. The bed was made, but she was gone."

Addison twisted the knob on the door, entered the room. "Her suitcase is still on the side of the bed. Wonder where she went."

"I think it's safe to assume wherever she is, she'll be back."

Addison raised a brow. "You say that like it's a good thing."

He smiled. "Depends on the day, I guess."

"I've been meaning to talk to you again about what happened the other night. I know how upset you were, and I just wanted to say again, I'm sorry. I should have trusted you."

He set the sack down on the kitchen counter. An apple slipped out, rolling across the counter until Luke snatched it up in his hand. "I know you're sorry about it all. I can see it in your face every time you look at me."

"Things haven't been the same since the other night. You've been great, a lot nicer than I deserve, but there's still a distance between us. I can feel it. When I woke up this morning, it crossed my mind that this life, who I am ... it might all be too much for you. Truth is, I'd understand if it was."

Luke cupped Addison's face in his hands. "Don't you know by now how much I love you? I'll always love you, always be here for you, no matter what happens."

Addison wrapped her arms around him. The front door burst open, and Marjorie strolled in. She looked at Luke and Addison and grinned. "Well, aren't you two a sight? If the lovefest is over, I'd like some breakfast, please."

CHAPTER 37

Addison sat next to Marjorie at the kitchen table. "Where were you earlier?"

"I went to see Milton," Marjorie said.

"How is he doing? Has he been charged?"

"I don't know. They wouldn't tell me anything, and they wouldn't let me see him. Said visiting hours aren't until eleven. Guess there's nothing left to do except wait and try again."

Addison wondered why Marjorie hadn't stayed there a few more hours and waited it out. "Can we talk about last night?"

"There's no need. I should have never treated you the way I did. You did what you thought was right. I can't blame you."

Addison rested a hand on Marjorie's wrist. "I didn't give Milton up. He gave himself up. He overheard the conversation I was having with Lia. She suspected foul play and planned on saying so in her report. I thought she might be bluffing, trying to see what I'd say. Milton obviously believed her and decided the jig was up."

"Did she say what she plans to include in her report?"

"She didn't. I believe she'll help Milton if she can."

Marjorie made a face like she found the idea of Lia's assistance hard to believe. "Why would she stick her neck out for him, a man she doesn't even know?"

"I don't believe she is doing it for him," Addison said. "I think she's doing it for me."

CHAPTER 38

Rick Snider reclined back on his patio chair, thumbed the cap off his third bottle of beer, and took a long, heavy swig. Over the past year, his belly had become so round he could rest a beer can on top of it like it was a miniature table for one. The light beer he was currently chugging had been his wife's idea, her polite way of saying he was becoming a fat lard without actually coming right out and saying it. Secretly, he despised her for it, seeing her coercion as female manipulation at its finest. Watching him drink the lower-calorie beer put a smile on her face. Put a smile on his too, because he understood something her dumb ass didn't. Her efforts to trim the fat hadn't done squat. If anything, they validated his indulgence in a few more beers per day than usual. After all, low calorie was less filling, right?

Rick kicked his feet up, resting them atop the plastic cooler in front of him. A pickup truck passed by. He watched it do a U-turn and roll to a stop at the edge of his driveway. A man and woman exited the vehicle. They were young, upper twenties maybe, or lower thirties. Too old to still be in college, he guessed. They didn't look familiar. So what were they doing walking across his front lawn?

Rick smacked a hand against his chest a few times to release the belches he'd sequestered and said, "You here about the puppies?"

"The puppies?" the woman asked.

She was smiling, flashing him a set of perfectly straight teeth, so straight he wondered if they might be veneers. Her shiny hair smelled like roses dipped in honey. He leaned forward, taking a nice, long whiff. "We only have the one boy left. All the girls sold yesterday."

"We're not here about the puppies."

"What are you here for then?"

"Are you Rick Snider?"

He nodded. "I'm Rick. Who are you?"

"My name's Addison, and this is Luke."

Luke tipped his head forward, said nothing, which Rick found disturbing. Why let the woman do all the talking?

"We'd like to talk to you about Vivian and Grace Clark," Addison said.

"Who?"

"The Clark girls, Rose and Clifford's kids. I know it's been awhile, but you were at the Easter party the night they fell from the window, weren't you?"

Meddlers. If he had known what they were after, he would have gone inside the house when they drove up, shut the door, locked it. Too late now. He set the beer down next to him and crossed his arms on top of his belly. It had been such a long time, he hardly remembered what the twins' names were anymore.

"I was there," he grunted. "So were a lot of other people."

He thought about asking them who they were, why they wanted to know. He decided against it, hoping the less he said, the faster they'd leave.

"Were you ever with the girls that night?"

"What do you mean *with* them? We weren't the same age. I wasn't friends with them. I was friends with their brother."

"So you didn't play hide-and-seek?"

"Hide-and-seek?"

"In the attic?"

Rick sat straight up. "Who are you?"

"A friend of Rose Clark."

He found this disturbing too. Why send kids to do her bidding? Wasn't like Rose. Not the Rose he remembered. "Why is Rose dragging all of this up again?"

"She has her reasons."

"Which are?"

"You never answered my question."

"Which question?" Rick asked.

"The one about you playing with the girls."

"No, I wasn't playing hide-and-seek. No, I wasn't with either one of the Clark girls. This subject was buried long ago. Best to leave it where it is."

"Best for whom?"

"I don't follow."

"What if I told you the Clark girls' deaths weren't an accident?"

Rick stood and turned, his arms flailing to the side to keep from losing his balance. Perhaps he'd had enough light beer for today. "I'd tell you you're crazy. You're both crazy. And you're wasting your time."

"Wait, if I could just ask you a few more questions. Please, it's important. If you could just hear me—"

"Get off my property or I'll call the police."

Rick entered the house, slamming the front door closed behind him. He walked to the kitchen table, shoving the mess aside until he found what he was looking for—his cell phone. Picking it up, he scrolled through the names trying to decide who he should call first: Derek or Dean.

CHAPTER 39

The difference between Rick Snider and Dean Roberston was like the difference between a carrot and a pea. Although both were in their mid-fifties, Rick's appearance was weathered and worn, while Dean, with his dark hair and tanned skin, didn't look a day over forty. Dressed in a tailored grey suit, a silk necktie, and manicured fingernails that gave Addison the urge to hide her own nails inside her pockets, it was obvious his physical appearance wasn't just important to him—it was everything.

Sitting in Luke's truck in a parking lot next to Dean's law firm, Addison watched Dean pace back and forth while talking on his cell phone. She wondered if it was Rick on the other end of the line, until Dean smacked his leg, threw his head back, and cackled like he'd just been given the world's funniest punch line.

"When he gets off the phone, I'd like to approach him on my own," Addison said.

"Not a chance," Luke replied.

"If you're sitting here watching our conversation, I'll be fine."

"I don't like it, Addison. It's not a good idea. We don't know anything about this guy."

"I promise I'll stay where you can see me. I won't go inside the building."

"How do you even know he's Dean Robertson?"

Addison raised a finger, pointing at the billboard next to Dean's office. It was a cheesy, larger-than-life picture of Dean's face, along with the caption: *You're not alone. We're in this together.*

Nice.

"This guy will do better if he's approached alone, and by a woman," Addison said.

"And you know this because ..."

"Before I met you, I dated guys just like him. All flash and flare and 'stroke my ego, baby'. Trust me, I'm fluent in high-powered attorney."

Luke shook his head. "Stay where I can see you. I mean it, Addison."

She gave Luke a military salute, which he didn't find amusing. She then exited the vehicle and crossed the street. Mission accomplished, she realized she'd been a bit too hasty. Dean was still chatting away like a gossipy school girl at a frat party. She loitered for a moment before spotting a bench. She walked over, sat down, and waited.

And waited.

And waited.

"Do you always nap outside buildings before going inside?"

Startled, Addison looked up, realizing she'd sat for so long she'd drifted off for a minute. Dean stood in front of her, arms crossed, head cocked to one side. Curious.

"Who said I planned on going inside?"

"This is the only building on the block. What else would you be doing here?"

"Waiting for you."

"For me?"

"You're Dean Robertson, aren't you?"

He reached up, loosened his necktie, bestowing her with his million-dollar grin. "Have we met before?

Nightclub, maybe? Did I ... give you my card or something?"

"I'm afraid not."

He fiddled with the end of his tie, thinking.

"You can relax," Addison said. "We haven't met."

Though he put on a brave, neutral face, the deep breath he took proved she'd put him at ease. "Do we have a meeting my assistant failed to tell me about?"

"I'm not a client."

He stroked his chin, grinned. "Tell me, Miss Not-a-Client, how long before we skip the shenanigans and cross the finish line?"

"Depends."

"On what?"

Addison leaned back, smiled. "How much time we have together."

"How much time would you like?"

Though she played it cool, the *thump, thump, thump* inside her chest proved otherwise. "How much are you offering?"

"Depends on why you're here, what you want from me. What you *really* want."

"I'm afraid it's not half as scandalous as you hoped."

He sat down next to her, so close their hips were touching. He glanced at his watch. "Well, if you're going to burst my 'woman of mystery' fantasy, you better get on with it. I have a *real* client in ten minutes."

Go time.

"My name is Addison Lockhart. I came here today hoping I could talk to you about Vivian and Grace Clark."

There was a long pause followed by a nod of understanding. "Why dance around it? Why not come right out and tell me why you were here in the first place?"

"Honestly? I thought if I did, you wouldn't talk to me."

"Have you looked in the mirror lately?"

Had she ... what?

"I don't know what you mean."

"You're stunning, Addison Lockhart. What man *wouldn't* talk to you?"

Plenty of men.

"You're not upset?" she asked.

"Why would I be?"

"You're not the first person I've talked to. It's not the most welcome topic. Believe me."

"I understand why there would be reservations. What happened back then was horrible. I can still see it in my mind like it was yesterday. I wish I couldn't. I *really* wish I couldn't. What's your interest in their story?"

"I'm friends with Rose Clark. She's been doing a lot of thinking about her daughters, about the night they died, how they died. I don't think she's ever stopped grieving, or wondering what really happened that night in the attic. What do you remember?"

He crossed one leg over the other, rested a hand on top. "Let's see. It was crowded, and loud. People everywhere. I was maybe fourteen at the time, or fifteen. The dinner setup was elaborate. Four long, rectangular tables in two rows. Ten or so at each table. Everyone ate dinner together. Once dinner was over, the adults separated from the kids. We had the run of the house, but we were warned to stay out of the main living room where the adults were drinking and carrying on."

"What did you do during that time?"

"The truth? I snuck into the kitchen when the servers weren't looking, took a bunch of glasses of alcohol off the trays. Then I went out back and drank it."

"Were you with anyone else?"

"Derek Clark and Rick Snider. Swiping the liquor was Rick's idea. He was the only one who'd ever had alcohol before. Derek and I were liquor virgins I guess you could say. Rick had four or five. Derek and I had maybe two or three each, which would be nothing now. But when you've never partaken of an adult beverage before …"

"So, you had a few drinks. What then?"

"Derek said he wanted to show us something in the attic. When we got to the door, it was locked. I thought that was it. Then Derek pulled out a key."

"Did he say why it was locked?"

"He didn't, but once we got inside, we had a pretty good idea. We followed him over to a box in the corner and opened it. Inside were stacks and stacks of *Playboy* magazines. He said they were his father's. He dug a bunch of them out and passed them around."

Dirty magazines. Now she knew what Vivian had found. Her face felt hot, sweaty. "When you looked at the magazines ... did you, uhh ... I mean, were you ... was anyone else up there with you at the time?"

He shook his head. "It was just the three of us at first. We were flipping pages, pointing and laughing at the pictures like the stupid teens we were. We were up there for about five minutes when we heard footsteps on the stairs. Derek thought it was his mom, coming up to bust us. We threw the magazines back in the box and slid it to the side. When the door opened, it wasn't his mom. It was Vivian and Grace. One of their bedrooms was right beneath the attic. They were playing together and heard us walking around."

"What did you do when you saw them?"

"What do you think we did? We panicked. Vivian said she knew we'd been drinking."

"How?"

"She'd spied on us earlier, saw us outside. It changed everything. The original plan was to go back to Derek's room and hang out until we felt normal again. And our parents had all been drinking so we figured there was no way they'd notice. When Vivian confessed, all we could think about was what we could do to keep those girls quiet."

"Keep them *quiet?*"

He raised a brow. "Bad choice of words. I know what you're thinking, and you're way off. The plan was to keep them occupied until we sobered up. Then it would be our word against theirs if it ever came out."

"So you all played hide-and-seek with the girls, right?"

He raised a brow. "How did you know?"

She ignored his question. "Did everyone play?"

"At first."

"The police report stated the girls were alone in the attic when they fell. I imagine you were all interviewed. Why lie?"

"We *didn't* lie."

"Then how did Vivian and Grace end up alone?"

"Rick and I distracted the girls while Derek went downstairs to make sure no one saw his sisters go up to the attic. Stupid idea. He ran into the cook. She knew the alcohol was missing and could tell by the way Derek was acting that he'd been drinking. She said Rick's mom had been looking all over for him."

"What did you do?"

"At first we thought if we all stayed in the attic, we'd be fine. But we knew Rick's mom wouldn't stop looking until she found him. And since he'd had the most to drink, we thought she'd tell everyone else's mom and we'd all get busted. Derek came up with a plan, and the three of us went downstairs together."

"You said three. What about the girls? They weren't with you?"

He shook his head. "We told them we'd be right back, and we meant it. Once we had everything under control, we planned on going back to the attic."

"Weren't you concerned they wouldn't stay up there?"

"We told them we were going to get some candy from the kitchen pantry, and if they wanted any, they needed to wait for us and to be quiet."

"What was Derek's plan?" Addison asked.

"To separate."

"Why?"

"He thought if we were apart, we had a better chance of convincing everyone we weren't up to anything. We made a deal that if one of us was caught, he wouldn't rat on the others. Derek went to his room,

Rick stuck about five sticks of chewing gum in his mouth and went to find his mom, and I found the closest bathroom and shut myself inside for a few minutes until it was time for us to meet back up again in the attic."

"And did you meet up again?"

"We didn't. Several minutes went by, and then I heard a woman scream. I peeked out the bathroom door. The adults were gasping and crying, and I heard someone say Vivian and Grace were dead."

"Do you remember seeing the doll that night—the one police found on the roof?"

"I don't. I mean, there were a lot of boxes up there, so it could have been anywhere." He paused for a moment then said, "Rose doesn't think it was an accident anymore, does she?"

"What do *you* think?"

"I'll admit I've gone over it in my mind many times over the years. The idea of their deaths being an accident has never sat well with me."

"Why not?"

"When I reached the bottom of the stairs that night, I saw this guy, Corey Finch, walk out of one of the bedrooms. He was zipping up his pants. A woman walked out behind him. She was older than he was. I don't know how much older, but I do know this—she was married, and not to Corey."

"What does that have to do with Vivian and Grace?"

"Vivian was a lurker. It was like every time I came around the corner, there she was. Watching. Observing. I mean, it's probably nothing, but what if she saw them together and they knew about it? Like I said, it's probably nothing."

"Why not tell the police your suspicions?"

"I was a stupid teenage kid. I didn't think anyone would believe me. And even if they did, there was never any proof they were involved."

Never any proof—yet.

Dean stood. "Well pretty lady, it's time for me to go. Give Rose my best when you see her, would you?"

Addison extended a hand. "I appreciate you taking the time to talk to me."

Dean reached inside his suit, handed Addison his business card, winked. "If you ever feel like getting together again, for drinks, or ... anything else, you know where to find me."

CHAPTER 40

Marjorie sat in the living room, a half empty glass of wine in hand, staring at the wall. When Addison and Luke came through the front door, she didn't budge or even blink. She just kept staring.

"Marjorie, are you okay?" Addison asked.

She leaned back, swallowed the remainder of the wine. "I will be. Eventually."

"Did you see Milton?"

"I did."

"And?"

"It's over. He confessed. Like he said before, he couldn't live knowing he'd lied about what happened."

"I'm sorry," Addison said.

"Don't be. Yesterday I thought protecting him was the right thing to do—the best thing. I was wrong. Seeing him today, he's in a better place. His conscience is clear."

"What happens now?"

"I've hired him an excellent lawyer. He'll be tried for assisted suicide under the euthanasia law. He'll likely face charges for second-degree manslaughter."

"What kind of time will he get if he's convicted?"

"Spoke to your friend while I was there. She went to see him too."

"Lia?"

Marjorie nodded. "She said the maximum sentence is fourteen years."

Fourteen years.

At Milton's age, Addison doubted he'd last more than ten.

"Does Lia think he'll receive such a long sentence?"

"She doesn't know. She did say she'd do whatever she could to help him. Since he's already talked to the police, she doesn't know how helpful she'll be, but she's determined to try."

A loud, thunderous pounding sounded. Someone was beating on the front door.

Luke held out a hand, preventing Addison from passing. "You better let me get it."

When the door was opened, a fired-up Derek stepped inside. He spotted Addison and pointed. "I knew there was something off about you. I *knew* it! I don't know what kind of scam you're running, or who the hell you *really* are, but you'd better stop filling my mother's head with delusions about your fake ability to communicate with my sisters. They're dead. End of story."

Marjorie shot up.

Luke pressed a hand against Derek's chest, pushing him backward. "If you want to have a civilized conversation, you can continue. If not, this is your warning to leave. Your *only* warning. You don't get to walk into our home and speak to Addison the way you are right now."

Derek pushed back. "You kiddin' me? I'll talk to you *and* I'll talk to her any way I like. You came into my home first, and now I'm dealing with my mother's nutty theories about my sisters being pushed out the attic window."

"What if they *were* pushed?" Addison asked. "Are you saying you've never once considered the possibility?"

Derek waved a finger around in the air. "Oh no, I'm not doing this. I see what's happening here. You're mad. You're *all* mad."

Marjorie approached, brandishing a finger of her own. "Are you really skeptical of Addison's abilities, or are you here because you're afraid?"

Derek pressed a hand to his gut and burst out laughing. "Afraid? Of what?"

"Of someone finding out what really happened the night the girls died," Addison said. "The story you *didn't* tell the cops."

"What story? There is no story."

"So you never got drunk with your friends? Never went into the attic and showed them your father's naughty magazines? Never played hide-and-seek with Vivian and Grace?"

"How did you ... who told you—"

"It doesn't matter. What matters is you withheld information from the police the night your sisters died to save yourself."

He shook his head. "I was downstairs when they died."

"In your room, right? What I'd like to know is, did anyone actually see you in your room, or did everyone just take your word for it?"

"What, you think I killed my own sisters?"

"I don't know. Did you?"

Expletives flew from Derek's mouth.

Luke shoved Derek out the front door and followed behind him, closing the door as he did so. Marjorie and Addison stood at the living room window, watching as the back-and-forth banter between the two men continued. It ended with Derek brandishing not one, but two middle fingers and then peeling out of the driveway in his father's antique car.

"Well, what do you think?" Marjorie asked. "Did he do it?"

Addison frowned. "I don't know. I just don't know."

CHAPTER 41

Corey Finch planted a kiss on his wife's cheek, grabbed the morning paper off the porch, and descended the entry steps leading to the driveway. His wife stood in her usual spot, the same spot she stood in every day when he left for work where she waited until he reversed out of the driveway before turning and going back into the house. Others may have viewed the daily ritual as mundane. To Corey it was endearing, a sign of their unwavering love for each other.

In another two months, he'd retire as manager of the local car dealership, and the life they knew would change forever. They'd sell the house, buy a Winnebago, and travel the world together. Nora had already been going through the houses, boxing things up they'd need and donating the rest to the thrift shop.

Halfway to his vehicle, he looked up, saw a man and a woman walking toward him.

"Can I help you folks?" he asked.

The woman and man introduced themselves. The woman, Addison, said some new information had come to light regarding the death of Vivian and Grace Clark—information she believed might lead to police reopening the investigation.

"Why would you want to talk to me about it?" Corey asked.

"Were you with someone at the party?"

"What do you mean—*with* someone? My parents were there."

Addison blushed. "You were seen with a woman the night of the party. An older woman. A married woman."

"What about it?"

Nora walked up beside him, and said, "Corey, what's going on?"

"This is Addison and Luke," Corey explained. "They said the cops might be looking into the deaths of Vivian and Grace Clark again."

Nora pressed a hand to her chest. "I still remember the look on her face when she found her girls the way she did."

"Wait, you were there?" Addison asked.

"I was," Nora said.

"Who are you?"

"Nora Finch."

"She's the, uhh, 'older woman' you mentioned a minute ago."

"But weren't you married to someone else?"

"I was," Nora said.

Addison glanced at Corey. "And weren't you a lot younger?"

"I was seventeen at the time. She was twenty-two. She'd just told her husband she wanted a divorce. By the time it was finalized and we married, I was nineteen. I'm sorry, what does any of this have to do with why you're here?"

"The night of Rose's dinner party, we were told the two of you were seen coming out of a bedroom together."

"It's possible."

"Not in a friendly way. In a compromising way."

"Meaning?" Corey asked.

"You were seen zipping up your pants."

Nora cupped a hand over her mouth, giggled. "How funny. I remember how sneaky we thought we were. Who saw us?"

"One of the teenagers."

"Yes, but who?" Nora pressed.

Corey clutched his wife's hand. "Honey, I don't think they want to name names."

A look of confusion swept across Nora's face. "Why not? Why does it matter now? We're married."

"You didn't come all this way to tell us we'd been outed for something we did forty years ago," Corey said. "What do you want, another statement? Do you realize how impossible it would be to recall any details now?"

Addison nodded. "You're right. I'm sorry for bothering you."

CHAPTER 42

Corey and Nora were married, an interesting detail Addison hadn't foreseen. She wondered if she'd made the right decision by not pressing them, pushing harder for more details. Nothing about them, not in their demeanor or their body language, gave her any reason to believe they were hiding something. Of course, they could have been. Some of the most cunning killers were also the calmest, the most charming. Case in point: Jeffrey Dahmer.

The more Addison thought about it, the more she convinced herself Derek, Rick, and Dean were at the heart of it all. But which one, or two, or all of them? What if they were protecting each other? And even more sinister, what if they were *all* in on it together?

Thirty minutes before, she'd called Rose, asking if she could stop by, see her alone, without Derek. Rose confessed she hadn't seen Derek since the previous morning. She didn't know when he would stop by again, but he wasn't there now. She didn't say a word about her son dropping by Addison's house the night before. Maybe she didn't know. Or if she did, she didn't mention it.

Before the call ended, Rose shifted the conversation to Rick and Dean, asking whether Addison had seen them. Addison filled her in on her conversations with both men, including her additional visit with Corey Finch. Although each conversation was productive in its own way, none provided what Rose really wanted, a definitive answer, the person responsible for the deaths of her daughters.

During her phone call with Rose, an idea occurred to Addison, something she wished she'd thought of all along. The more she thought about it, the more she convinced herself she'd found the perfect way to get the answers to everything.

CHAPTER 43

Rose ushered Addison and Luke inside the house and closed the door. "What do you want with the doll?"

"Do you still have it?" Addison asked.

"It's here somewhere. Haven't seen it in years."

"I need to know how it got on the roof, who put it there, and why."

"Seeing the doll won't give you those answers."

Addison raised a brow, smiled. "It might."

"Wait a minute. You're hoping you'll touch it and see something, aren't you?"

"It's worth a try."

Rose left the room, returning several minutes later, doll in hand. She held it out to Addison. Addison hesitated, her eyes fixed on the freakish-looking toy dangling from Rose's hand. As dolls went, it wasn't what she expected. Naked and minus an eyeball, its coarse red hair made it look like a prop from an old horror film.

"Go on," Rose said, shaking the doll at Addison. "Take it. What are you waiting for?"

What *was* she waiting for?

It was weird having an audience, standing there, staring at her, even if the audience included someone as familiar as Luke. She sat on the center of the sofa. "Will you place it in my lap? There's no telling what will happen when I touch it. Most of the time when I touch something, I'm taken off guard. I'd like to be prepared."

Rose shrugged like she found the request trite, but did as Addison requested.

The old woman was hunched over like an exuberant teen with a front-row seat to the freak show, making Addison uncomfortable. Luke seemed to pick up on this and suggested they back off, give Addison her space.

Rose turned and moved next to Luke. "Right, right. Sorry. I don't mean to brood."

Addison closed her eyes and pressed her hands into the stomach of the doll. She waited several seconds then opened her eyes again.

"Well, what did you see?" Rose asked.

"Nothing."

"What do you mean nothing? You couldn't see who threw the doll onto the roof?"

"I mean, I didn't have a vision. When I touched the doll, nothing happened."

"It was your first try," Rose said. "Maybe you need to let go and try again."

Addison shook her head. "If something is supposed to happen, it always does."

Rose breathed a disappointed sigh. "What now?"

A thought occurred to Addison. "When the police found the doll, did it look the same way it does now?"

"It had on the dress it came with when I bought it," Rose said. "Blue with flowers."

"Where's the dress now?"

"Why does the dress matter?"

"If the person who threw the doll touched the dress, it's the dress I need."

Rose glanced to the side, thinking. "It wasn't in the box with the doll. The only other place it could be is in a box in the storage shed. I don't like going into the shed. Too many insects and spiders crawling around."

"Why don't I come with you?" Luke suggested. "You tell me where the boxes are, and I'll go in and get them."

"Fair enough," Rose replied.

"If you do find it, I don't want to try this again out here," Addison said. "I think I'll have better luck in the attic where it all happened."

"You can go on up if you like." Rose winked. "It's been unlocked since the night you broke in."

CHAPTER 44

Addison pushed the attic door open and stepped inside the room, the slats of old wood creaking beneath her feet as she crossed to the window and glanced outside. In the daylight, the view was much different. Looking down, it was easy to see just how far of a fall it was. How terrified the girls must have been.

Not wanting to catch her finger on another fragment of frayed wood, she kept her arms folded in front of her. Looking at the window frame, she noticed something. The wood slat lining the window was only splintered in one place, the area around the rusty nail. She bent down. Not only was the wood splintered, a chunk the size of a nickel was missing, and what she'd previously assumed was rust on the head of the nail now didn't look like rust at all. It was brown and dark, almost like a stain. The nail's head was sharp and gnarly, the metal looking like it would leave a lasting impression upon contact. A lasting impression. Possibly even a scar.

Addison took out her cell phone and dialed.

"I've been meaning to call you all day," Lia said. "About Milton, I'm sorry. I tried. I really did."

"I know, and it's okay. Listen, I have a question."

"Shoot."

"If a person cut themselves forty years ago on a nail, what would the blood on that nail look like today?"

"I'd have to see it to be sure, but it would be brown in color and have the appearance of dirt or rust."

"Could it be tested for DNA?"

"If the blood has decayed, then no, it can't. To test blood from the seventies, it would depend on how well it was preserved, protected from the elements. Addison, what have you found?"

"Possible blood on a nail in the Clarks' attic—a nail on the window the girls fell from."

"Then it's probably their blood. I can come over, see if I'm able to extract any usable DNA. I've always hoped one day I could reprocess the attic."

"I think I know who did it. I think I know who's responsible for killing Vivian and Grace."

The attic door creaked open. Addison turned around. A man walked in. A man she hadn't seen before. He was bald and muscular, like a heavyweight boxer. In his right hand, he held a pistol.

"Put the phone down."

Addison lowered her arm, but kept the phone in her hand.

"Don't be stupid," he said. "End the call."

She didn't move.

For the second time in this room, a gun was pointed her direction. Through clenched teeth, the man said, "End. The. Call."

Voice trembling, Addison replied, "Why? You're going to kill me anyway, aren't you? Isn't that why you're here?"

The sound of his thick, black boots boomed across the room. He snatched her phone and dropped it on the floor, smashing it beneath his foot.

"You Addison?"

"Yes," she squeaked. "Where's Rose? Where's Luke?"

"Don't worry about them."

"How did you know where to find me?"

"Been tailing you all day."

"Who are you?" she asked.

"Don't matter."

"Why are you here?"

"Why you think?"

"To clean up."

"Clean up. Yeah, somethin' like that."

"Why send you? Why not do it himself?"

He roared with laughter. "Squeamish, I guess. Don't wanna get his hands dirty."

"People hire you to kill other people?"

"I'm hired for a lot of things. Like you said, when there's a mess, I clean it up."

"And how many messes have you cleaned up for *him*?"

"A few. This is the first time he's asked me to kill for him, though. I usually just intimidate, break a few bones."

"Do you even know why he hired you? Do you care?"

"Look, lady. What's done is done. Turn around."

"What?"

"Turn your freakin' head around and face the wall, or I'll shoot you in the face."

Vivian and Grace appeared, one on each side of Addison. Their mouths opened, and in unison, a chilling scream was emitted into the air. The windowpane shattered, then burst shooting fragments of glass throughout the room. Addison dropped to her knees. The floorboards beneath the man's feet came unhinged, and he lost his footing. The pistol slipped from his hands, skidding across the floor. They both scrambled for it, Addison almost grabbing hold before the man snatched it up again. He whirled the pistol toward her and fired.

CHAPTER 45

Addison opened her eyes. The bald man was on the floor beside her, his head drowning in a pool of blood. She arced around, looked up. "Derek?"

He leaned Rose's rifle against the wall and extended a hand, pulling her back on her feet. "Are you all right?"

"I ... think so." A wave of panic gripped her. "Derek ... your mother! Luke! The man said, I mean, I don't know, but we have to—"

Derek placed a hand on her wrist. "It's okay. They're all right. This man, whoever he is, locked them in the shed out back. I ran to the house to get the key to let them out and heard the window shatter."

"You saved my life."

Derek spread his arms to the side. "What in the hell happened in here anyway? Who is this guy? Why was he trying to kill you?"

"I need to see Luke," Addison said. "Please. I have to know he's all right. Then I'll tell you. I'll tell you everything."

Sirens howled up the road, vehicles screeching to a stop in front of the manor. An army of footsteps ascended the stairs. Officer North led the way, his eyes bulging in disbelief when he realized the woman standing in front of him was the same woman he'd arrested at this same house before. "You, again?"

Addison half waved. "Uhh, hi."

Lia sprung into the room, elbowing Officer North aside. She threw her arms around Addison. "You're alive!"

A minute later, Luke and Rose had been freed, and they too entered the room. Luke pulled Addison to the side, planting a kiss on her lips. "I thought I lost you."

Officer North rolled his eyes. "Okay, people. Everybody out. This is a crime scene, not a drive-in movie theater. Move this little reunion of yours somewhere else."

CHAPTER 46

Several hours later, police had enough evidence to detain Dean Robertson for solicitation of murder. After searching through the bald man's phone history, several calls were found both to and from Dean's number. A stone-faced Derek sat silently on a chair in the library where everyone had gathered, a look on his face like he was still in shock. Although they hadn't kept in touch over the years, in his youth, Dean had been one of his closest friends.

"After all this, we still don't know what happened," Marjorie said.

"We know enough," Addison replied.

"Enough to help my girls move on?"

Still the nonbeliever, Derek rolled his eyes.

"With your permission, I'd like to try," Addison said.

"Can I be in the room with you? Can I speak to them one last time?"

"You wouldn't be able to see them even if you were there, Rose. I'm sorry."

"Doesn't seem fair, does it? Can you at least tell them something for me?"

"Anything."

"Tell them I love them. Tell them I think of them every day. All I want now is for us to be together again."

Addison smiled. "Believe me, they know."

...

Marjorie and Addison sat in the center of the attic, legs crossed, hands clasped together.

"Go ahead," Marjorie prompted. "You do the honors this time."

"Are you sure? Last time you—"

Marjorie squeezed Addison's hand. "One day, you'll have your own daughter, and I won't be here. It will be up to you to teach her. Now close your eyes and let him come. It's time."

"Clifford Clark, we invite you in," Addison said.

Bright light exploded into the room, a white sphere, bathing the room in an effulgent glow. It dissipated, and the celestial body of Cliff Clark emerged. He looked around, at the room, at Marjorie and Addison. "Who are you? Where am I?"

"You know where you are," Addison said. "Take a minute. Try to remember this place."

His eyes came to rest on the shattered window. "I'm ... this was my home. My daughters ... they ... I can't find them."

"Good," Marjorie said. "He knows where he is, and he's been looking for his daughters. Let's reunite them."

"Vivian and Grace Clark, we invite you in."

Vivian appeared.

"Where's Grace?" Addison asked.

Vivian angled her head toward the coat closet. After all they'd been through, Addison had hoped Grace would come willingly this time.

"I need you to open the door to the closet," Addison whispered. "I need you to take her hand and force her out, Vivian. You're the only one who can."

"But I—"

"Now, Vivian. It needs to happen now."

Vivian half opened the door, peeked inside. "Grace, we have to go now."

"I won't leave Mama. She's all alone."

Vivian reached a hand inside the closet, helped Grace out. Grace stood motionless, her eyes closed. "Open your eyes, Grace. It's Daddy. He came back for us."

"What's happening?" Cliff asked. "Where are my daughters?"

Addison looked at Marjorie. "Why can't he see them?"

"He can't see them, and they can't cross until Grace accepts what happened to her."

Grace opened her eyes. "Daddy? Daddy?"

"Do you want to be with him?" Addison asked. "Do you want him to see you?"

Grace nodded.

"Then I need you to be brave, just for a minute. Okay?"

She nodded, again.

"The night you died, you were playing hide-and-seek in this room, weren't you?"

"Uh-huh."

"Vivian found some pages from a magazine, and she ran to the window. Do you remember what happened next?"

Grace wriggled her hand free from Vivian's, walked to the window, looked down. "Vivian! No!" She curled her fingers, began clawing at the open air, like she was trying to keep an invisible force away from attacking her.

"I think she's reliving the moment after Vivian died," Addison said.

"She's dead!" Grace screamed. "You killed her! You killed Vivian! I'm telling!"

Vivian ran to the window, seized Grace by the arms. "It's okay. I'm here. It's over. He can't hurt you now."

A single tear seeped from Cliff's eye. Arms extended, he said, "Vivian? Grace?"

Grace turned. "Daddy?"

She'd finally seen what she needed to see. Both girls ran to their father, who enveloped them in his arms. Reconciliation complete, their spirits started to fade from the room.

Vivian looked at Addison and smiled.

Grace said, "Tell Mama we know what she said. Tell her we love her."

Cliff clutched his daughters in his arms, looked at Addison and Marjorie, and said, "I don't know who you are, but thank you."

And then they were gone.

CHAPTER 47

The following morning, Lia granted Addison a favor. A quick favor. Five minutes with a man who was currently in police custody.

"I heard you confessed," Addison said.

Dean Robertson glanced up. "Guess I'm a lousy criminal."

"Guess so."

"Tell me, how did you figure out it was me? When did you know?"

"I didn't. Not until I found the dried blood on the nail and remembered shaking your hand yesterday and seeing that nasty scar on the inside of your palm, right below your thumb."

"Could have happened any number of ways."

"But it didn't," she said. "And when the DNA test comes back, it will be a match."

"It doesn't matter if it's a match or not. I confessed."

"Why now?"

"After what happened last night, I knew the investigation would be reopened. Besides, it was time."

"It was time, or you were given an ultimatum to confess?"

"I don't follow."

"I received an interesting call this morning," Addison said, "from your old pal Rick. Want to know what he told me?"

"I can't imagine."

"He told me he called you last night, right before you were arrested, and said if you didn't confess, he'd confess for you. Guess you should be more careful about the things you say to someone when you're drunk."

"Guess so."

"You hired someone to kill me."

Dean walked to the front of the cell. "You're wrong. I never told him to kill you. I told him to scare you. He took it too far."

"Nice story. Did it convince the police? Because you sure as hell aren't convincing me."

"It's the truth. Why would I lie now? I'm a lawyer. I know what I'm facing."

"It could be worse. You could be dead like Vivian and Grace."

"It was an accident, you know? One of the guys at the party needed to use the bathroom, and I didn't know where else to go. I decided I'd go back to the attic, wait for the guys there."

"Vivian ran to the window, flung the magazine pictures around. You were embarrassed. You tried to get them from her, but your body weight was too much, and she fell."

Dean stepped back, his face filled with confusion. "What you just said is more detail than I admitted to the police. How could you possibly know? Vivian and Grace were the only ones in the attic besides me."

"What I don't understand is, how did Grace end up sharing the same fate? How did the doll end up on the roof?"

"It's all in the police report."

"I don't want to read it in a police report or see it on the news. I want you to tell me."

Dean sat back down, burying his head in his hands. "When Vivian fell, Grace tried to escape, to run downstairs. I knew what would happen. I knew she'd tell. I dragged her to the window and pushed her."

"And the doll?"

"I saw it sitting there in a box. I pulled it out and chucked it on the roof."

"So the cops would think the girls had risked their lives trying to get it."

"I never thought it would work. When it did, I couldn't believe it."

"How is it no one saw you leave the attic?"

"They were all outside. By the time they stormed the attic, I had blended in like I'd been standing there with everyone the whole time."

"You won't understand what I'm about to say, but you have no idea the damage you've done. Not just with Vivian and Grace's deaths, but after. It's a shame New York doesn't have the death penalty anymore. You deserve it."

Addison turned, headed for the door.

"Wait."

"No," she said. "We're done here."

"I had a dream last night. Vivian and Grace were hovering over me. They grabbed me, hauled me across a bunch of broken glass over to the window. They lifted me by my collar like I weighed nothing and tossed me out. It was so real, like it was really happening. And you want to know the weirdest part? I didn't find out about the shattered window until this morning."

Addison smirked. Maybe the girls were getting sweet justice after all.

She turned around. "That dream you had—if I were you I'd get used to it."

CHAPTER 48

Three Months Later

Addison plopped down on the sofa next to Luke and said, "Ready?"

He reached for the remote and frowned.

"Oh, come on," Addison joked. "You lost the bet. It's *one* chick flick. I think you'll survive."

"Yes, but a period film?"

"*Sense and Sensibility* is my favorite. You did say *any* movie."

He bumped her shoulder with his own. "Yeah, because I was sure I'd win."

"I'll make you a deal. *Sense and Sensibility* today, *American Sniper* tomorrow."

The television screen sprung to life, and the previews began.

Addison stood.

"Where are you going?" Luke asked. "You just sat down."

"Forgot my blanket."

"While you're up, could you get me something?"

"Sure."

"Some Ben & Jerry's."

She grinned. "You mean *my* Ben & Jerry's?"

He laughed. "Don't be stingy. I'll buy you another pint tomorrow."

"I'm going to hold you to it."

"Oh hey, I forgot to ask—how was your visit with Milton today?"

"Good. He's letting Marjorie live in the house Helen left him while he serves his time."

"What is his lawyer saying? Anything new?"

"He's hopeful they'll put him on probation, give him community service soon. He'll still be in there for a while, but hopefully not too long. I have to say, he amazes me."

"The lawyer?"

"Milton. I never had the chance to get to know him before now. In a way, he's like the grandfather I never had. Our visits mean so much to him. I think they fill some of the void he feels over losing Helen."

Addison went to her room and removed the afghan from the end of the bed, crunching the soft layers together beneath her nose. She breathed in. The red and white afghan was one her mother had crocheted for her years earlier. Every once in a while, she still caught a lingering whiff of her mother's perfume. It seemed silly, but it kept her close somehow.

Blanket cloaked around her, she descended the stairs, noticing Luke was no longer on the couch. She called his name. He didn't respond. Thinking he'd gone to retrieve the ice cream himself, she went to the kitchen. He wasn't there. She opened the freezer and glanced around, not seeing her usual flavor of ice cream on the shelf where she usually left it. Pushing a few slabs of meat to the side, she spotted the pint container all the way to the back, wedged between a few other items. She reached a hand inside, gripped the tub, and pulled forward, realizing it was light. Much too light. She closed the freezer door and looked down, noticing the label looked different than it normally did. Instead of the purple "Chocolate Therapy" she was used to, in big, red lettering it said, "Will You Marry Me?"

"Addison?"

Eyes blurred with tears, she turned.

Luke was lowered on one knee, holding a velvet box in his outstretched hand. He popped the box open, revealing the sparkly diamond inside. "Addison Lockhart, the day you came into my life was the first time I ever had a desire to spend my life with someone else, to have a family, to grow old with someone by my side. And I knew I'd never be truly complete until I was yours, and you were mine. Will you marry me?"

Unable to speak, she nodded. Luke slipped the ring on her quivering finger, stood, and pulled her toward him, sealing the deal with a gentle kiss.

"It's a yes, right?" he asked.

"It's a yes," she replied. "It's always been yes."

THE END

Sign up for Cheryl Bradshaw's Killer Newsletter today and receive a FREE eBook.
Learn more at www.cherylbradshaw.com

...

All of Cheryl Bradshaw's novels are heavily researched, proofed, edited, and professionally formatted by a skilled team of professionals. Should you find any errors, please contact the author directly. Her assistant will forward the issue(s) to the publisher. It's our goal to present you with the best possible reading experience, and we appreciate your help in making that happen. You can contact the author through her website, www.cherylbradshaw.com.

...

About Cheryl Bradshaw

Cheryl Bradshaw is a *New York Times* and *USA Today* bestselling author writing in the genres of mystery, thriller, paranormal suspense, and romantic suspense. Her novel *Stranger in Town* (Sloane Monroe series #4) was a 2013 Shamus Award finalist for Best PI Novel of the Year, and her novel *I Have a Secret* (Sloane Monroe series #3) was a 2013 eFestival of Words winner for best thriller.

Learn More:

Blog

cherylbradshawbooks.blogspot.com

Web

www.cherylbradshaw.com

Facebook

www.facebook.com/CherylBradshawBooks

Twitter

www.twitter.com/cherylbradshaw

Cheryl Bradshaw's Author Newsletter

www.formstack.com/forms/?1369010-ZIjE9iGjGY

Enjoy the Story?

You can show your appreciation by leaving a review on Amazon, Barnes & Noble, iBooks, Google play, or in the Kobo Store. If you do write a review, please be sure to email Cheryl at cherylbradshawbooks@hotmail.com so she can express her gratitude.

Books by Cheryl Bradshaw

Sloane Monroe Series
Black Diamond Death
Murder in Mind
I Have a Secret
Stranger in Town
Bed of Bones
Hush Now Baby

Addison Lockhart Series
Grayson Manor Haunting
Rosecliff Manor Haunting

Till Death do us Part Novella Series
Whispers of Murder
Echoes of Murder

Boxed Sets
Sloane Monroe Series (Books 1-3)
Sloane Monroe Series (Books 4-5)
Till Death do us Part (Books 1-2)

Printed in Great Britain
by Amazon